"Your son is not the only one of royal blood. You are Princess Sarina de Valmont."

Sarah's legs felt like jelly. "Every adopted child wonders if she's really a princess.... Does that make us cousins?"

Josquin shook his head. "Are you disappointed that we're not related?" he asked.

She would have been more disappointed if they had been. She wasn't sure why, because she had no romantic interest in him. "Why should I care either way?" she asked carefully.

A shadow darkened Josquin's handsome features. "When we met, I sensed a connection between us."

She wasn't about to admit that she had felt it, too. "You've just said we're not related by blood."

"There are other kinds of connections between a man and a woman."

Dear Reader,

What makes readers love Silhouette Romance? Fans who have sent mail and participated on our www.eHarlequin.com community bulletin boards say they enjoy the heart-thumping emotion, the noble strength of the heroines, the truly heroic nature of the men—all in a quick yet satisfying read. I couldn't have said it better!

This month we have some fantastic series for you. Bestselling author Lindsay McKenna visits use with *The Will To Love* (SR 1618), the latest in her thrilling cross-line adventure MORGAN'S MERCENARIES: ULTIMATE RESCUE. Jodi O'Donnell treats us with her BRIDGEWATER BACHELORS title, *The Rancher's Promise* (SR 1619), about sworn family enemies who fight the dangerous attraction sizzling between them.

You must pick up *For the Taking* (SR 1620) by Lilian Darcy. In this A TALE OF THE SEA, the last of the lost royal siblings comes home. And if that isn't dramatic enough, in Valerie Parv's *Crowns and a Cradle* (SR 1621), part of THE CARRAMER LEGACY, a struggling single mom discovers she's a princess!

Finishing off the month are Myrna Mackenzie's *The Billionaire's Bargain* (SR 1622)—the second book in the latest WEDDING AUCTION series—about a most tempting purchase. And *The Sheriff's 6-Year-Old Secret* (SR 1623) is Donna Clayton's tearjerker.

I hope you enjoy this month's selection. Be sure to drop us a line or visit our Web site to let us know what we're doing right—and any particular favorite topics you want to revisit. Happy reading!

Mary-Theresa Hussey

Mary-Theresa Hussey
Senior Editor

Please address questions and book requests to:
Silhouette Reader Service
U.S.: 3010 Walden Ave., P.O. Box 1325, Buffalo, NY 14269
Canadian: P.O. Box 609, Fort Erie, Ont. L2A 5X3

Crowns and
a Cradle

VALERIE PARV

SILHOUETTE *Romance*

Published by Silhouette Books

America's Publisher of Contemporary Romance

To Mary-Theresa Hussey,
whose enthusiasm for Carramer earns her
honorary citizenship, with appreciation from the
Carramer royal family and their historian.

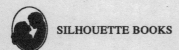 **SILHOUETTE BOOKS**

ISBN 0-373-19621-0

CROWNS AND A CRADLE

Copyright © 2002 by Valerie Parv

This edition published by arrangement with Harlequin Books S.A.

Visit Silhouette at www.eHarlequin.com

Printed in U.S.A.

Books by Valerie Parv

VALERIE PARV

lives and breathes romance, and has even written a guide to being romantic, crediting her cartoonist husband of nearly thirty years as her inspiration. As a former buffalo and crocodile hunter in Australia's Northern Territory, he's ready-made hero material, she says.

When not writing about her novels and nonfiction books, or speaking about romance on Australian radio and television, Valerie enjoys dollhouses, being a *Star Trek* fan and playing with food (in cooking, that is). Valerie agrees with actor Nichelle Nichols, who said, "The difference between fantasy and fact is that fantasy simply hasn't happened yet."

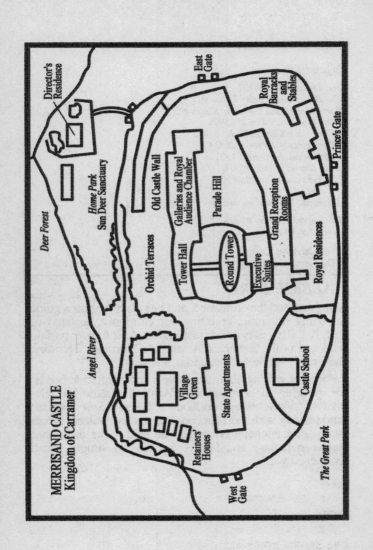

MERRISAND CASTLE
Kingdom of Carramer

Prologue

Prince Josquin de Marigny had been careful not to let a look or gesture betray how restless he felt. But his close friend, Peter Dassel, who chaired the Carramer Business Consortium of which Josquin was patron, leaned closer and murmured into his ear, "Now you've shown the flag and presented the awards, you're wondering how soon you can get away, aren't you?"

The reception for outstanding Carramer business people had already run over its allotted time in the prince's schedule, thanks to the lengthy acceptance speeches the winners had chosen to give. Now they milled around Château de Valmont's beautiful East Salon, enjoying coffee, delicious pastries and the opportunity to network with one another. No wonder they weren't anxious to depart.

Josquin restrained a sigh. "I didn't mean to let it show."

Peter shook his head. "It doesn't except to me, Josh. I've known you a long time."

Since they had attended the same school, Josquin thought. They had met within months of their eighth birthdays. As the son of the Australian ambassador to Carramer, Peter had refused to be intimidated by Josquin's title or his close relationship to the ruling family of Carramer. Peter had challenged Josquin to a running race to prove that the Australian was the prince's equal. Not accustomed to being challenged by a commoner, Josquin had accepted. Over a distance twice as long as Peter had originally proposed, they had raced to a hard-fought draw, and afterward had become firm friends. Josquin had been delighted when Peter had taken out Carramer citizenship, and their friendship had grown stronger over the years since then.

Now Peter gave an understanding grin and said in a lowered voice, "I hope she's beautiful."

Josquin's coffee cup stilled in midair and he frowned. "Who?"

"The woman you're so anxious to get away to meet."

Josquin lowered the cup and deposited it on the tray of a passing waiter. "How do you know there's a woman involved?"

"I don't, but I live in hope. Good grief, Josh, you're thirty next month. Isn't it time you settled down?"

"Maybe I like playing the field."

"And maybe you're too fussy for your own good."

"You realize it's high treason to talk to a member of the royal family this way?"

Peter made an unconvincing attempt to look alarmed. "Somebody has to talk to you this way. Your quest to restore your family's lands and fortune is commendable. But at the rate you're going, you'll be a venerable forty before you let any woman get past your guard, far less anywhere near the altar."

Josquin nodded pleasantly to one of the award recipients, but was thinking of his self-imposed timetable. Until he had more to offer a woman, he didn't plan on getting romantically involved with anyone. "Forty isn't too old for marriage these days."

"Depends whether you want to have the stamina to keep up with the little princes and princesses when they come along. Personally I prefer having my children while I'm still young enough to enjoy them."

As godfather to Peter's three-year-old son and one-year-old daughter, Josquin was inclined to agree. He felt a wintry expression settle on his face. "We can't all be as lucky as you."

"Lucky, nothing. The day I set eyes on Alyce, I knew she was the one for me. I mapped out a campaign to win her, and the rest was history."

"Did she know how calculating you are?"

Peter laughed. "She knew. I found out later that she had the same idea." His expression sobered. "Jokes aside, Josh, when you finally meet the woman for you, I hope you won't let pride stand in your way."

His friend turned to speak to another guest, leaving his words hanging around Josquin like a cloud. It was easy for Peter to talk. His parents hadn't squandered everything they had as if there was no tomorrow. Fleur, his mother, a former lady-in-waiting at the court of Prince Henry, ruler of Valmont Province, had taken to her role as a princess like a duck to water. Indulged by Josquin's father, Leon, who could refuse her nothing, Fleur had run up accounts everywhere as if the royal coffers had no limits, until Leon was forced to sell most of the family's land holdings to pay their way.

But for the patronage of Prince Henry, who had treated Josquin like a son, Josquin would have had a struggle to complete his education. Whenever he thought of the difference the elderly ruler had made to his life, he felt a debt of gratitude. Prince Henry had had no obligation to nurture Josquin. He had a father, however improvident, and Josquin wasn't related to Henry. But Henry's own son had died in his twenties, leaving a breach in the ruler's life that Josquin knew he had helped to fill. It was little enough repayment for all Henry had done for him over the years, helping to compensate for the benign neglect Josquin's parents had shown their only son.

Josquin hadn't learned the full extent of their feck-lessness until he was twenty-three, when his father suffered a fatal heart attack, leaving almost nothing except the remnants of the family estate on the outskirts of the capital city of Solano. Josquin quickly realized that his mother couldn't cope on her own, and expected him to manage her life for her.

He had put in years of hard work and careful management before they could breathe easily again. Even now his mother's lifestyle could hardly be called frugal although she complained about what she called her reduced circumstances. She had no idea what it cost Josquin even to keep her in clothes, far less maintain her household in Solano. Money seemed to flow through her hands like water. She was hardly an ideal advertisement for married life.

All the same, he found his thoughts turning to the woman Peter had accurately guessed Josquin was anxious to meet as soon as his work here was done. He knew the woman well enough to be able to pick her out of a crowd, knew her history, her habits and lifestyle, her tastes in clothing and food, as well as if they had been married for years. Odd to think that he was about to meet her face-to-face for the first time.

Sarah McInnes was the name she was known by in America. Her name conjured in Josquin's mind the image of a startlingly beautiful woman in her mid-twenties. She had long hair the color of nutmeg, curling softly onto her shoulders, and dark brown eyes that reminded him of the rare and beautiful sun deer running wild in the forests of Carramer.

By now Josquin had seen enough photographs of her to guess that if she stood alongside him, she would come up to his chin in her stocking feet. The reports said she had trained as a dancer in her early teens until she grew too tall to become a ballerina, and had entered the art world as an assistant curator after leaving college. He had little trouble imagining how she would move, with a dancer's easy grace.

Two years ago, she had moved out of the apartment she had occupied in her parents' home, and now lived alone. Not quite alone. Josquin frowned as he thought of the baby Sarah had given birth to almost a year ago. There was no sign of the child's father, and Josquin's investigators had been unable to identify him. The prince felt himself tense involuntarily as he thought of Sarah managing entirely alone since her child's birth. He had spent too much of his childhood fending for himself while his parents were wrapped up in their own lives, not to empathize with her struggle.

He was curious as to what had caused the break between herself and her American family. She hadn't become pregnant until after she left home, ruling out the baby as the cause. According to the reports, Sarah had taken very little with her when she left the McInnes household, and her present lifestyle was far from lavish.

Yet Josquin could only admire the life she had made for herself and her child.

Since the investigators had tracked her down a few months ago, Josquin had followed Sarah's progress avidly. With every new report he became more fascinated by her, and more intrigued at the prospect of finally meeting her. If he hadn't been determined not to get involved with any woman, his preoccupation with her would have been a real concern.

He glanced at the Rolex on his wrist. Where was his equerry who had been instructed to interrupt if the function went on too long? On cue, Gerard appeared at the door, his gaze sweeping the room until he located Josquin. Approaching the prince, the equerry bowed deferentially and announced, "Your Highness, your next appointment is waiting for you."

Not a moment too soon, Josquin thought. He gave Peter an apologetic look. "If you'll excuse me, duty calls."

Peter inclined his head respectfully, but Josquin caught a gleam in his friend's eye. "Thank you for supporting our work, Your Highness. Appreciated as always," he said. Under his breath, Peter added, "When you meet your mystery woman, don't do anything I wouldn't do."

Josquin resisted reminding his friend how much scope that would give him if he took it literally. Peter had been far from saintly until marriage settled him down. Nor did Josquin bother denying that there was a woman involved. He would only fuel Peter's suspicion.

He let his equerry clear a path for him through the crowd, nodding and smiling his way to the door and heaving a sigh of relief when it whispered shut behind him. These functions were good for the province's economy, and as Prince Henry's principal business adviser, Josquin willingly supported them, but the benefits didn't stop the social side from boring the pants off him.

Unlike the meeting that lay ahead of him.

A smile tugged at his mouth as he anticipated meeting Sarah in the flesh at last. He knew how beautiful she was, and how she lived, but he wanted to know what she was really *like*. Would she be as charming in person as she had looked when the photographer had captured her playing with her baby on a blanket in a park near her apartment? She had been unaware of being observed, and the delightfully unselfconscious way she looked was imprinted on Josquin's memory.

He sobered abruptly as his thoughts strayed beyond the initial meeting. Not for the first time, he wished that Henry hadn't insisted that Josquin be the one to find her and have her brought to Carramer. After everything the old prince had done for him Josquin could hardly refuse, but he couldn't make himself feel good about it. He wouldn't be the only one when Sarah found out what Henry expected of her, Josquin thought, as he waited for his car and driver to take him to their meeting.

Chapter One

Sarah McInnes bounced the grumbling baby on her hip. "Not much longer now, little one." She nudged her suitcase forward with her foot, frowning at the slow-moving line ahead of her. The Carramer people might be "the world's most delightful hosts" according to the brochures, but their customs officials had scant regard for a baby's needs. Christophe was tired after the long flight and she could see him getting ready to give his small lungs a workout.

She was being ungrateful, she knew. She was about to visit one of the most beautiful countries in the world, thanks to a radio station's computer that had dialed her phone number at random in a competition. Given the odds against winning such a wonderful prize, how could she feel unhappy about anything? She put her mood down to exhaustion. Although the flight attendants had been wonderful, taking turns to distract him, Christophe had fretted most of the way from America. As a result Sarah had slept little herself.

Suddenly her attention was captured by a flurry of activity at the station ahead of her. A handsome man strode up to the officials and spoke quietly to them. Their response, instant and unmistakably deferential, made her wonder who the man was and why everyone jumped to attention when he appeared on the scene.

She had sworn off men, even ones with hair the color of midnight and the build of an athlete straining his designer suit. He would never be able to buy clothes off the rack, she thought, not with those wide shoulders and narrow waist. From where she stood she couldn't see his legs, but as he had crossed the customs hall, the men with him had struggled to keep up.

The man's intense gaze swung to the people in her line. Was it her imagination, or did his gaze rest longer on her than on the people around her? There was no reason for her to be singled out. She was only an ordinary tourist visiting the country. A different line catered for people traveling on business visas, so none of the people around her could be tycoons planning to pour millions of dollars into the island kingdom's economy, especially not Sarah herself.

For someone who had no interest in men other than the adorable one-year-old in her arms, Sarah found herself paying a foolish amount of heed to the way everyone danced attendance on this one man. He stabbed a finger at the computer screen alongside him and began to talk in a lowered voice.

Only another customs official, she concluded. Maybe he was simply one of those men who commanded attention no matter what their position in life.

Since she wasn't going anywhere in a hurry, she amused herself by continuing to study him covertly. She put his age at about thirty, although it was hard to pin down when he moved with such athletic grace. When he finally strode away, she felt something very like disappointment.

She was startled when a uniformed man approached and placed a hand on her shoulder. "Kindly come this way, madame."

His tone carried a hint of command, and her stomach lurched. Had she made a mistake when she completed the entry formalities for herself and Christophe? Sarah had never been in trouble of any kind, and had never been to Carramer before. While studying the brochures, she'd felt drawn to the place, but put the feeling down to her lifelong fascination with the South Pacific. So what could be the matter?

She decided she wasn't giving up her place in line without some explanation. "I'm sure you mean to help," she said firmly. "But I'm almost at the head of the line and if I lose my place now, it will be hard on my baby. He's already tired and fractious."

As if to confirm her assertion, Christophe gave vent to a series of escalating wails that had the soldier wincing in sympathy.

"The child is the reason we wish to expedite your entry," he said over Christophe's cries. "Please come with me."

Since she was the only person in line carrying a baby, the officials must have felt sorry for her. Who was she to argue with anything that speeded this up? Aware of the curious glances of the people remaining in line, she allowed the soldier to pick up her suitcase, and followed him across the customs hall to a pair of wood-paneled doors. He swung one of them open, put her case down inside, and held the door wide so she could enter.

The activity had diverted Christophe, she was relieved

to see. His tears had dried to distressed hiccups, and he was looking around curiously. The peace wouldn't last but she was grateful for the respite.

Before the door closed, she saw the soldier take up a post outside—to keep her in, or others out? Then the heavy door swung completely shut and the sounds of the reception hall melted into silence. All she could hear was the sound of her own fast breathing. Plush carpeting masked the tentative steps she took into the room.

"Please come in and take a seat."

She hadn't been imagining things, the intriguing man from the customs hall *had* paid her special attention. He was doing it now, she saw as she approached the massive antique desk he was seated behind. A leather folder lay open in front of him and she was alarmed to see that her photo lay on top of a thick sheaf of papers. Not her passport photo, either. This one showed her with Christophe in the park opposite their apartment. What was it doing here, and how did this intriguing stranger come to have it in his possession?

She perched on the edge of a leather sofa in front of the desk, settling Christophe on her knee where he began to play with the amber beads around her neck. "Would you mind telling me what this is all about?"

"First I need to confirm a few details. May I see your passport, please? The baby's, too."

She handed them to him. "Is something wrong?"

"Nothing's wrong, I assure you. This will only take a moment."

In spite of his assurance, her apprehension grew as he studied the documents. She told herself that his manner was pleasant enough. Surely if there was a problem, he wouldn't keep glancing from the passports to her, as if she intrigued him for some reason.

Her peace of mind wasn't eased by the awareness that he was more startlingly good looking up close than he had seemed from a distance. His eyes were the gold-flecked blue of a stormy sea, and his skin was lightly tanned, emphasizing her first impression of him as the athletic type. It wasn't hard to imagine him on the bridge of a yacht, fighting the helm for mastery of the waves. His commanding presence suggested he would win.

Since she was studying him she could hardly feel insulted at finding herself on the receiving end of an equally thorough inspection. If she didn't feel so uncertain as to why he had singled her out, she would have been flattered.

"Your full name is Sarah Maureen McInnes, and your baby is Christophe Charles...McInnes?" he said.

Hearing the slight upward inflection in his voice, she frowned. "I'm a single mother, if that's what you mean," she said.

"I'm merely checking facts. No judgment is implied," he said.

She immediately regretted reacting so defensively. Just because other people had drawn unflattering if inaccurate conclusions about why she was single with a baby, didn't mean everyone was the same. "I'm tired. Christophe is tired. We've had a long flight," she said by way of mitigation. "I'd like to know what's going on, Mr.—" she read the brass nameplate at the front of the desk "—Mr. Sancerre."

The corners of the man's mouth twitched. "Forgive me for not introducing myself right away. My name is Josquin de Marigny. The airport director, Leon Sancerre, kindly permitted me the use of his office for this meeting."

Iced water skittered along her spine, as she recalled a

fragment of information from the tourist brochures. "De Marigny? Isn't that...aren't they..."

"The royal house of Carramer," he supplied.

She was glad she was already seated. Her knees felt as if they would buckle if she tried to stand. No wonder everyone had deferred to him. What on earth was going on here? "Are you the king?" she asked in a strangled voice.

He shook his head. "By tradition, Carramer has no king. Our present ruler is Prince Lorne de Marigny, my cousin," he added before she could frame the question. "I serve as an adviser to Prince Henry de Valmont, ruler of Valmont Province. According to these documents, Valmont is your destination."

She was too busy dealing with her confusion, to absorb the details. "Look, Mr....that is, Your Highness, I won this vacation in a contest, and the destination was Valmont Province. I had no say in it, although from all accounts it's one of the most beautiful parts of Carramer. But I'd still like to know what you want with me."

"Ah yes, the contest. Did it not occur to you to wonder how you came to be so fortunate?"

"When you haven't had a vacation in two years, and a radio station calls to say a computer has awarded you a trip to a fairy-tale South Pacific kingdom, and all the documentation arrives in your mailbox as promised, you don't look a gift horse in the mouth."

She felt her heart sink as the obvious thought occurred to her. "Are you trying to say I *didn't* win a contest? Was it some kind of hoax? Is that why you had me removed from the line?"

He shook his head. "You're right, there was no contest. I arranged for the call to be made as a way to bring you to Carramer."

Clutching Christophe tightly to her, she struggled upright, so disappointed that she hadn't won a trip after all that she didn't care whom she offended. Prince or not, he had no right to play with her life. "I don't know what's going and I don't care anymore, but I'm calling the police. I'm sure this is against some law or other even in Carramer."

With all the grace and speed of a leopard, the prince moved to her side, urging her to sit down again. This time, he took a seat beside her, keeping his hand on her arm. "Hear me out first, then you may do whatever you feel you must, although the American police won't be much help now you're on Carramer soil."

"Am I a prisoner here?"

"The opposite in fact. You belong here as much as I do."

She felt the floor drop away beneath her feet and was glad of his touch to anchor her in reality. She had dreamed of this moment for nearly two years, yet suddenly she felt afraid. "Do you know who I am?"

He paused long enough for her heart to begin a frantic tattoo. "I believe so."

She could hardly breathe for the tension coiling through her. She tightened her hold on Christophe. "Tell me," she implored in a voice barely above a whisper.

The prince's firm grip on her other arm sent a silent message of support. "My searches suggest that you are a citizen of Carramer."

"You mean I was born here?"

"No, you were born in America."

"Then how can I..."

"There are a few minor details to be confirmed, but I'm already sure I have the right woman."

"The right woman for what?" She may not be who

she had grown up thinking she was, the child of James McInnes, the well-known Californian property developer, and his artist wife, Rose, but she didn't think she was from anywhere like Carramer, either.

"You do know you were adopted soon after your birth?" the prince prompted.

Her voice came out as a strangled whisper. "I found out when I had a blood test for a persistent virus two years ago. The hospital said I couldn't possibly be my father's child. At first I thought my mother might have had an affair, but then I discovered that I didn't belong to her, either."

"Surely a birth certificate was required when you obtained your passport?"

"That was an excellent forgery, too, although I didn't know it." She had obtained her passport for a vacation in Europe to celebrate her graduation. She hadn't known the truth about herself then, and had never doubted that her documents were authentic. Her adoptive parents' wealth had its uses, she had concluded. If it could buy them a child, obtaining false documentation for her was a minor detail.

"You were never told the circumstances of your birth?"

She shook her head. "They didn't want me to know I was adopted. When I found out, and wanted to look for my birth parents, James refused to help me. He said I would have to choose between them and him." Her voice cracked. "He reminded me of all they had done for me, and told me I should let the past lie. Do you know what that past might be?"

The prince nodded. "What I have to tell you may take some time, and I would prefer a more appropriate setting."

"Why can't you tell me now?"

"It would be better if you weren't glancing at your watch every few minutes."

She had been unaware she was doing it. "Christophe needs to be fed and changed and put down for a nap," she said. Not to mention that she needed rest herself. His suggestion that he could tell her about her background had temporarily banished her own tiredness, but it would catch up with her later, she knew.

"Then I will escort you to your accommodation," he said as indecision gripped her. "We can continue our discussion after you attend to your child."

She thought of the contrast between his life as a prince, and hers as a single mother. "I hope you're prepared for a culture shock," she said shakily.

He looked amused. "Prince Lorne has two young children, as does his brother Michel and their sister, Princess Adrienne. I've had ample practice at taking care of my cousins' babies."

"Don't princes have servants to take care of the less pleasant chores?"

He hesitated before saying, "Some do."

But not him, she heard the implication. Why not? Was he a modern royal who preferred to do things himself? Given his personal intervention in her affairs, it seemed so. She curbed her impatience. "Why can't you just tell me what you know?"

"There is every chance that you will refuse to believe me. I need time to convince you to trust me."

Oddly enough she was inclined to do so already, she realized, wondering at the same time why she did. It wasn't because he was a prince. She'd read enough about royalty to know they suffered from the same human weaknesses as everyone else. Something about Prince Josquin himself inspired her trust.

As he used the phone to summon a car for them, she watched him in fascination. He was obviously accustomed to being in a position of power. She saw it in the relaxed way he gave orders, as if he expected them to be obeyed. Without question.

Her gaze was riveted by the way he rested a muscular thigh on the edge of the desk, letting one leg swing free. He looked like a man who was comfortable with his position in life, she thought. Since she had no idea what her position in life was, having had all her assumptions turned on their heads by the discovery that she was adopted, she couldn't help envying the prince his air of self-assurance.

His eyes were half closed, veiling their unusual color under a sweep of lashes that matched the blue-black of his hair. His lean, aristocratic features had probably taken generations of breeding to achieve such a prepossessing result. Her heart picked up speed again. What kind of breeding had produced *her?*

The prince knew the answer but she sensed he wouldn't tell her until he judged the time was right. She saw intrigue in the gaze he turned on her as he dealt with the call. Intrigue and something far more disquieting, a fire she had last seen in a man's eyes the night Christophe had been conceived. Recalling the life-changing impact of that experience, she felt her internal temperature soar. She fussed with Christophe's clothes, not wanting Josquin to see how badly his gaze had unsettled her.

He barely knew her. Then she thought of the thick file in the prince's possession. He must know a lot more about her than she did about him. More than she knew about herself, come to that.

Her first clear memory was of her third birthday party at the McInnes home in Southern California. Brendan, the boy next door, had taken her red balloon and burst it in her face when she asked for it back. She was wary of balloons to this day. She had been an above-average student and model daughter, bowing to her father's wish that she attend a local college so she could continue to live at home.

She was twenty-seven and a Libran, celebrating her birthday on September 29, as far as she knew. Now she wondered if she could trust anything she had been told about herself all her life.

She still felt like the same person inside. Still the same stubborn, opinionated, deliver-on-your-promises woman she'd always been. Three-year-old Brendan had found out to his cost when she threatened to punch his nose if he didn't return her balloon. He had burst it so she had punched his nose. She had spent time standing in the corner afterward, but the pattern had been set. She still did what she said she would do, no matter what it cost her.

A shiver took her. She felt more adrift now than when she had learned of her adoption. The prince had no right to make her wait for information that concerned her so intimately. But as a grown woman, she could hardly threaten to punch him in the nose, so she schooled herself to patience. She had a feeling he wasn't a man she could hurry into anything.

"How did you know I was arriving today?" she asked as Josquin opened the door to escort her to the car. Stupid question, she thought. He had obviously arranged everything. She was still shaken to discover that the vacation she thought she'd won was nothing more than a hoax, but she wasn't as furious with him as she thought she should be.

"I was waiting for you," he confirmed. At his slight gesture, a porter sprang to their side. At the prince's quiet instruction, the man retrieved her suitcase and carried it away. She watched him go with some trepidation, realizing that she had placed herself and her child entirely in the prince's hands.

Christophe had dozed off at last, not waking as they left the airport building. He slept with his head on her shoulder, one thumb anchored in his mouth and the other clutching a fistful of her shirt. With any luck he wouldn't stir until they reached their hotel, if that's where the prince was taking her.

"You've gone to a lot of trouble to get me here. I must be somebody important," she said, striving for lightness and failing. "Why did you have to lure me to Carramer to speak to me?"

"Because we are running out of time."

"You know you're driving me crazy?"

His stern mouth softened into a slight curve. "I can't say I mind having that effect on such a beautiful woman."

She resisted the urge to feel complimented. "I'll bet you say that to lots of women."

"Would it surprise you if I deny it?"

She nodded. "I'd have trouble believing it."

"I shall take that as a compliment. Here's our car."

She stopped in her tracks, astonished to find a chauffeur opening the door of a black stretch limousine for her. What she took to be the royal standard fluttered from the hood. This would raise a few eyebrows if it were to pull up outside her apartment block in North Hollywood, she thought.

She had been the recipient of enough barbed comments when her neighbors discovered she was a single mother with a baby and no sign of a father. It was a pity they wouldn't get the chance to see this. She smiled.

The prince looked at her curiously. "What do you find so amusing?"

"I was picturing the reaction back home if I rolled up in this. You're used to it, I suppose."

His gaze lingered on her face. "Not so used to it that I can't enjoy it through your eyes."

She made herself comfortable on leather upholstery that felt like riding on a cloud. One seat held a baby capsule with a pristine lambswool lining. Without waking him, she secured Christophe in the seat, unnerved at this evidence of how thoroughly the prince had prepared for their arrival.

The compartment was fitted with a television screen and a well-stocked bar. As the car glided out of the airport, the prince deftly opened a bottle of French champagne, and poured the golden liquid into flutes. He handed one to her. "To your safe arrival."

She drank to quiet her screaming nerves, feeling anything but safe. It dawned on her that she had allowed herself to be talked into riding in a car with a complete stranger, just the situation her parents—that Rose and James, she amended mentally—had warned her against when she was growing up.

They had wanted her to be perfect. Perfection had always been paramount to James McInnes, whether in his business or his private life. If he could have adopted a boy so easily, he probably would have done so. As it was, Sarah felt sure he hadn't told her she was adopted so he wouldn't have to acknowledge what he saw as a shortcoming. He had probably regarded her wish to search for her birth parents as a criticism of himself as a father. He refused to accept that this wasn't about him or Rose, but about Sarah and her needs. Rose McInnes had been more understanding, but as always, followed her husband's lead.

Getting pregnant hadn't been Sarah's intention, but she had felt so cut adrift by their lack of support, that she had turned to her childhood friend, Jon Harrington, for comfort. Neither of them had counted on compassion turning into passion and then into something beyond their control, but it had.

What a combination. She hadn't been sure which of them had been the least experienced, little Miss Perfect or Jon, the would-be priest. Inexperience hadn't stopped them from creating a child between them. Her breath caught as she looked at the baby sleeping, lulled by the limousine's smooth motion. Christophe was the most precious thing in her life, the only person to whom she truly belonged. She regretted her lack of self-control with Jon, but she could never bring herself to regret the child they had created.

Jon never knew he had fathered a child and he never would, if she had anything to do with it. If he knew, he would insist on taking responsibility, even marrying her if she wanted him to. But he had dreamed of becoming a priest for as long as she could recall, and she was determined not to take his dream away from him. She felt badly enough having her own life in ruins thanks to James McInnes. She wasn't about to ruin Jon's life as well.

Soon after she discovered she was pregnant, Jon had entered the seminary, and their contact had been limited to letters every few weeks. In his last letter, he'd told her he was being sent to his order's mission in South America. She missed his friendship, but the loss was a small price to pay to let him hold on to his dream. When Christophe was old enough, she would tell him about his father, making sure her son understood what a special man Jon was.

She had found herself an apartment, supporting herself through her pregnancy and afterward with money from a trust fund left to her by her maternal grandmother. She and her grandmother had loved one another dearly, and she was glad her grandmother had died without knowing that they weren't related by blood after all. Sarah hadn't been in touch with her adoptive parents since she left, and she wondered with some bitterness, if they preferred it that way.

She took a sip of the champagne, feeling the bubbles tease her throat. She felt foolish worrying about what Rose and James would think of her behavior now, when she hadn't told them about her pregnancy. In any case, the man at her side wasn't a complete stranger. The soldier at the customs hall had called him Your Highness, and she'd bet that this car wasn't made available to just anyone. "It occurs to me that I should have asked to see some identification," she said.

The prince's deeply carved features relaxed into a look of amusement. "Perhaps my driver's license will do?"

"I didn't know princes had them."

He sighed, suggesting that he had had this conversation more than once before. "We put our pants on one leg at a time just like everybody else."

Don't even go there, she warned herself, as images of the prince getting dressed in the morning sprang to her mind. He was a means to an end, finding out who she was. Once he told her what he knew about her background, their paths might never cross again.

Strange how disappointing the notion felt, although she told herself it was to be expected. He was a member of the Carramer royal family, for goodness' sake. Once he had fulfilled whatever duty he had toward her, he wouldn't involve himself with the personal concerns of an ordinary citizen, assuming she was one. She couldn't suppress a feeling of anticipation at the prospect. For nearly two years after finding out that she was adopted, she had wondered where she fitted in. She had never considered that she might belong somewhere other than in America.

"Why are you taking such an interest in me?" she asked, giving voice to the thought she had suppressed since he singled her out for attention. "I'm not some royal love child, am I?"

"Are you always so persistent?" he asked, an edge in his voice.

Her throat dried. She had asked out of a perverse wish to provoke him, not because she thought that it could be true. Now she felt the ground shift under her again. What was so terrible about her background that he evaded her questions?

She twisted sideways, fixing him with her most imperious glare. He might be royal but she had been brought up as the daughter of wealthy parents. She wasn't intimidated by him, and it was time he knew it. "I insist that you tell me what you know about my background."

He seemed unmoved by her anger. "You'll have your answers very soon. We have arrived at your accommodation."

The car swung past a sentry box, a uniformed guard saluting as they drove between black wrought iron gates bearing enameled crests. The car continued along an avenue of ancient trees, through which she glimpsed palatial houses, suggesting that they had entered an exclusive enclave.

Before she could ask Prince Josquin, the car came to a halt beneath a sandstone portico. The building behind it was enormous, at least four stories high and spreading out in two wings for the length of a city block. By craning her neck she could make out a blue and jade flag fluttering from a mast atop a crenellated tower. Suspicion gripped her. "This doesn't look like a hotel. It looks more like…"

"Château de Valmont," the prince cut in smoothly. "Welcome home."

A scowl marred his even features, suggesting that no wasn't a word he was accustomed to hearing. After a thoughtful pause, he said, "Because your son is the heir to everything you see around you."

She felt the color drain from her face. "He's what?"

"He is Prince Henry's sole male heir."

"If it's true, it would make my baby...he would be..." She couldn't bring herself to force the word out.

Josquin did it for her. "He is Prince Christophe de Valmont."

Josquin saw the moment when her knees threatened to buckle. His strong arm came around her, supporting her and Christophe. She shook her head slightly to dispel the mist tugging at the edge of her thoughts. "There must be some mistake. We're American citizens. How can my son be the heir to anything in Carramer, far less a prince?"

"I understand this is a lot to take in. That's why I wanted to break it to you in a more appropriate fashion."

"Would any way make a difference when you have such news? Are you sure?"

Josquin inclined his head. "Too much is at stake for my inquiries to have been anything but meticulous."

They would have been anyway, she assumed. Josquin didn't strike her as a man who did anything by halves. She was far from convinced that the château was her son's birthright, but for his sake, she had to find out. "We'll come inside, for now at least," she said, keeping a tremor out of her voice with an effort.

The prince looked relieved. He indicated a pretty dark-haired woman of about Sarah's age, who had come to stand beside them. "This is Marie. She will serve as your personal attendant while you're here."

Which wouldn't be very long if Sarah had any say in

it, she thought as she greeted Marie. The longer she stood in the shadow of the breathtaking château, the more she believed that Josquin must be mistaken. The prince's research might have been thorough, but he would have to depend on advisers and investigators. Their information could have been wrong. It would be sorted out soon, then she and Christophe could go home.

There was no holiday. Belatedly she realized that the check she had received as spending money was as much a sham as the prize she had supposedly won. She would have to return the money to Josquin, although she had no idea how she was going to manage it.

"What if this turns out to be a mistake?" she asked.

He made a gracious gesture. "Then I will be the one who made it. You are welcome to remain at Valmont as a guest of the royal family for as long as you choose. It is the least I can do to make amends, *if* a mistake has been made." His tone said he doubted it.

Relief swept through her. Until now, she hadn't realized how much she had counted on this vacation to give her the chance to regroup. Although it had been her choice and she wouldn't change it for anything, bearing Christophe alone hadn't been easy. Her grandmother's legacy wouldn't last much longer. Soon she would have to return to work.

Her former job as assistant manager of an art gallery had been kept open while she was on maternity leave. With a baby to consider, she couldn't work the long, sometimes unpredictable hours she'd done previously, so she had been forced to hand in her resignation. She had intended to use her vacation time to plan her future.

"Thank you," she said, her tone betraying her relief.

The prince inclined his head. "You're welcome. Shall we go in now?"

A butler held one of the carved double doors open for her and gestured deferentially for Sarah to precede him.

Sarah found herself standing on a floor made of Italian travertine inlaid with granite. A coffered ceiling stretched twenty or more feet above her head. At one end of the cavernous hall was a wide, curving staircase.

Sarah had been surrounded by beautiful possessions all her life, but had seen nothing like Château de Valmont. "This is amazing."

"This is one of the finest houses in Carramer."

"I can believe it. Now I'm convinced you have the wrong person." Her son couldn't possibly be the heir to all this.

"Then I shall have to convince you otherwise."

"If it means living in such a magnificent place, I don't mind you trying."

At the excitement in her voice, he smiled. "The château stands at the center of a very large estate which is home to several members of the royal family. Substantial as the estate is, there are other royal homes that are even more impressive, such as the palace at the capital, Solano, home of the monarch, Prince Lorne."

"I can't believe it could be grander than this. Do you live here?"

"When my work requires it." He gestured for her to accompany him up the grand staircase.

The heavily carpeted treads made her feel uncertain— or was it the presence of the enigmatic man at her side? Either way, she was glad of the ornate balustrade to steady herself. Soon she would discover who she really was, and how her baby came to be a prince of Carramer, if that's who he really was.

Marie must have taken a route reserved for the servants, because she was already fussing over Sarah's suitcase when Josquin opened the door onto a lavish suite of rooms. "I hope you'll be comfortable here," he said.

Sarah had never seen anything like the suite spread out before her. Two bedrooms opened off a circular sitting area. Beyond it was a covered patio with a panoramic view all the way to the sea. The sun sparkled off an expanse of white sand that begged to be explored. Sarah hugged Christophe, making a silent promise to show him the beach. She couldn't wait to build his very first sand castle.

Marie carried some of Sarah's clothes into what turned out to be a walk-in closet, also with an ocean view.

"Comfortable? We may move in here for good," she said.

Josquin's mouth twitched. "Be careful what you wish for, Sarina."

She eyed him curiously. "What did you call me?"

"A local variation of your name," he said easily. "Does it trouble you?"

"I suppose not." More troubling was her feeling that his use of the name hadn't been entirely fortuitous. She wished he would tell her what he knew of her background and get this over with, but she sensed that Prince Josquin would do things in his own way and time.

She turned to the maid. "Marie, which is the baby's room?"

"It's all right, Marie. I'll take care of this."

The maid bobbed a curtsy, and Josquin opened a connecting door onto a spacious bedroom equipped with everything a baby could possibly need. Sarah settled Christophe onto a changing table beside an exquisitely decorated antique crib. Above it was a mobile of horses. She set them twirling. This was a far cry from the tiny bedroom she had turned into a nursery in her apartment back home, and she found herself wishing that her friends from the art gallery were here to see this.

Josquin angled his lithe body against the door frame and watched. Christophe reached for the mobile, kicking his legs in delight. "Horee, horee," he chortled.

"They sure are, sweetheart," she said, dodging flying feet as she set about changing him. "What a clever boy you are." So far his vocabulary had been restricted to bowie, his word for the bottle he had recently started to use, and her favorite word, Mama.

She buried her face against his tummy, blowing a raspberry against his velvet skin. "I love every one of your words, don't I? One day we'll have long talks and you'll tell me I don't know anything because I'm only your mother, so I'd better enjoy horee while I can."

Josquin looked intrigued. "He's already starting to speak?"

She looked up. "First words at one, sentences at two."

"So my cousins tell me."

"You don't have children of your own?"

"I'm not married."

She wasn't sure why, but the information lifted her spirits. "As a de Marigny, don't you have to take care of the succession or something?"

"Prince Lorne and Prince Michel both have sons, so the succession isn't something I need worry about."

She felt her eyebrows lift. "No daughters?"

"Women do succeed to the throne under some circumstances, but it is more usual in Carramer for titles to pass down through the male line."

She looked at Christophe. "Like the Valmont one?"

He nodded, and she added, "How can you be sure you have the right child?"

Josquin shifted slightly. "You took a DNA test once."

"That's right. It's how I discovered I was adopted." A horrible thought occurred to her. "You gained access to my medical records? How could you?"

"It was necessary."

"You had no right."

"I had a duty," the prince cut across her. "I may not approve of the investigator's methods, but I needed answers quickly."

She lifted Christophe off the table and sat down with him on a rocker placed beside the crib. The baby pawed at her breast but she hesitated. She had fed him discreetly in public before without feeling self-conscious about it, but she wasn't sure she wanted to do it in front of Prince Josquin.

He solved the problem by pacing to the window and looking out, keeping his back to her. She unbuttoned her blouse and Christophe began to feed eagerly. She felt the tug as an emotional pull deep inside her. But the contentment that usually accompanied it eluded her today.

She kept her voice low as she said, "You mentioned a time problem before. What did you mean?"

The prince kept his back to her. "Prince Henry has a serious heart condition with an unpredictable prognosis. He wishes to see his heir securely settled in Carramer in case the worst should happen."

Settled. How long had it been since she'd felt settled anywhere? She shifted Christophe to her other side. "I'm sorry about Prince Henry's ill health," she said,

"But your plan has a rather permanent sound to it. What if I decide not to stay?"

"Then you are free to leave."

She heard the tension in the prince's voice and wondered what he wasn't telling her. "You still haven't told me what you know about my parents," she said.

He swung back and froze, apparently riveted by the sight of her feeding Christophe. His voice sounded husky as he said, "Your father was Henry's only son, Philippe de Valmont."

She heard only one word. "Was?"

"He died in a waterskiing mishap soon after you were born. He never knew he had a daughter."

"And my mother?"

"Her name is Juliet Coghlan."

Sarah drew a sharp breath. "My father's secretary?" Sarah had known the woman through her childhood, without suspecting that they could be mother and daughter. Suddenly she understood why Juliet had been so affectionate toward her, giving her small gifts and treats, and making time for her, no matter how busy she had been.

Sarah remembered visiting her father's office to find him and his secretary in the midst of a blazing argument. Uncharacteristic tears had streamed down Juliet's face as she stormed out of the inner office. She had come up short at the sight of the distressed seven-year-old, but had refused to tell her what was wrong. Now Sarah wondered if she had been the focus of the disagreement.

Juliet had left the next day. There had been no calls or letters since, and James McInnes had told Sarah he didn't know where his former secretary had gone.

"Prince Philippe met Juliet when she was holidaying

in Carramer. They fell in love and sought Prince Henry's permission to marry," Josquin said.

Christophe had drifted off to sleep and didn't stir when Sarah tucked him into one arm. Feeling unusually self-conscious, she adjusted her clothing with the other. "I gather Prince Henry refused to give them his blessing."

"He wanted his son to marry a Carramer woman of his choosing."

"What happened?"

"Philippe told his father that he intended to renounce his title and follow Juliet to America. The love affair continued until she discovered what he meant to do. Evidently she didn't want him giving up everything on her account, so she pretended that the affair was over. She expected Philippe to return to Carramer and resume his royal duties."

This was her father, her real father. A man who had so loved her mother that he had been willing to give up everything for her. "Did he come back to Carramer?"

"For a time. He and Henry were barely on speaking terms, but Philippe did his duty to the letter, although everyone who knew him could see that his heart belonged elsewhere."

"How did you know he'd fathered a child, if he didn't?"

The prince reached into his pocket and withdrew a slim leather wallet. From it, he extracted a photograph that he handed to her. "Through this."

The air fled from her lungs as she looked at the photograph. "It's a picture of me." A similar one had stood atop the piano of her adoptive home for as long as she could remember.

"Read what's written on the back."

Sarah turned the picture over. The handwriting was Juliet's. "'My darling, I thought I could do this alone, but I need you. Our daughter needs you. Tell me what I should do.'" It was signed, "'Jay.'"

Sarah looked up at Josquin, feeling tears stain her cheeks. How could her real father have turned his back on such an appeal? "I thought you said Philippe didn't know about me."

Josquin took the photograph from her and returned it to his wallet. "He didn't. The photograph was delivered to his office an hour after he left to go waterskiing with friends. After returning from America, he was frequently preoccupied, and that day his mind wasn't on what he was doing. Another vessel ran him down. Philippe died on the way to the hospital. He never saw the photograph."

"Surely someone contacted Juliet to tell her what had happened?"

"Philippe's staff didn't know who Jay was, and Prince Henry was unapproachable for months after the accident. I think he blamed himself for Philippe's state of mind."

"He *was* to blame," she said hotly. "If he hadn't hounded the lovers, they'd have married and lived happily together." With her, she thought. Henry was responsible for destroying three lives including hers.

"Try not to think too harshly of your grandfather," Josquin urged. "He's from the old school, and believed he was doing what was best for the province."

"Don't call that horrible man my grandfather. From the sound of him, Christophe and I are better off not having anything to do with him."

Josquin gave a tight smile. "From what I've heard about him, you sound a lot like Philippe."

''I should probably take that as a compliment.''

She stood up and lifted Christophe against her shoulder. He gave a most unregal burp, then settled back to sleep again. He didn't waken when she placed him in the beautiful antique crib and tucked a soft blanket around him. Her heart swelled with love as she looked down at him. She couldn't imagine treating her son as heartlessly as Henry had treated Philippe.

''You still haven't explained how I came to be adopted,'' she said, turning back to Josquin.

''As far as we know, it was arranged privately through Juliet's association with your father.''

Sarah couldn't keep the bitterness out of her voice. ''Illegally, you mean?''

''Probably. There is no official record of the adoption. We assume that when she didn't hear from Philippe, Juliet decided that he didn't want to acknowledge their child. She already had an invalid mother depending on her and couldn't cope with more. Your father and mother wanted a baby but they were unable to have children of their own. When James McInnes found out what a struggle Juliet was having, he persuaded her that it would be kinder to you if she let him adopt you. As his employee, she was able to see you on an almost weekly basis.''

Sarah thought about the argument between Juliet and her father. ''All would have been well as long as my mother hadn't insisted that I be told who I was. She had a blazing row with my adoptive father. I'd say that was the reason. She left soon afterward. When I asked where she'd gone, I was told nobody knew.''

''We were not able to establish her whereabouts, either,'' Josquin said. ''I'm sorry.''

Bleakness gripped Sarah as she faced the possibility that her mother might have died. Now she would never know that Philippe hadn't abandoned her, or Sarah herself. Her only consolation came from knowing that her real mother had tried to do her best for her daughter.

"You do realize what this means?" Josquin said. "Your son is not the only one of royal blood. You are in fact, Her Royal Highness, Princess Sarina de Valmont."

Her knees jellied. "Every adopted child wonders if she's really a princess." Before he could respond, she added, "Does that make us cousins?"

He shook his head. "I'm from the de Marigny line."

"Then how can Prince Henry of Valmont be your uncle?"

"It's a courtesy title. He took over my education in my midteens when my parents proved less than adept at it."

She didn't miss the bitterness in his voice, and sensed that there was more to his admission, but he didn't seem inclined to elaborate.

"Are you disappointed that we're not related?" he asked.

She would have been more disappointed if they had been. She wasn't sure why, because she had no romantic interest in him. If anything, she should despise him because of his loyalty to Prince Henry, the man who had destroyed her real family. "Why should I care either way?" she asked carefully.

A shadow darkened Josquin's handsome features. "When we met, I sensed a connection between us."

She wasn't about to admit that she had felt it, too. "You've just said we're not related by blood."

"There are other kinds of connection between a man and a woman."

She threaded her fingers through the bars of Christophe's crib as an anchor. "I'm not looking for a connection, as you put it. I want to take my child and go home."

"You would deny your son his birthright because yours was denied to you?"

"I'm not doing any such thing." At least she hoped that wasn't her motivation. She made a sweeping gesture around the lavishly furnished suite. "None of this has anything to do with us. I'm half-American, remember? If what you tell me is true, Christophe has less Carramer blood in his veins than I do."

"Are you running away from his heritage, or from me?"

The prince's question stopped her in her tracks. "I don't know what you mean."

His dark gaze caught and held her. "Don't you? You deny feeling any connection between us, but it is there. I think you're afraid if you acknowledge it, you'll lose your head the way your mother did."

Sarah could hardly breathe for the emotions swirling through her. "It didn't work out all that well for her."

His hand came up and touched the side of her face. "Then consider this your chance to rewrite history."

She had to fight to resist the urge to turn her face into his hand. "You're assuming I want to."

"Oh, you want to."

How did he know, when she could barely explain her feelings to herself? Was such arrogant assurance a part of his royal heritage? If so, why didn't she feel as sure of herself? "Are you sure I'm a real princess?" she asked.

He looked mystified. "I guarantee it."

"Then let me issue my first decree. Take your royal hand off me now."

Chapter Three

Josquin took his hand away slowly, making it obvious that it was his choice rather than in response to her decree. "You're tired. You should rest."

"Rest won't change anything." Especially not the confused way she felt around him. "I want to go home."

"You are home, although I can understand if it hasn't sunk in yet. If you won't rest, come for a walk with me. I'll show you around the grounds of the château."

Going anywhere with him wasn't on her agenda, but she saw the sense in taking a walk. The long flight coupled with the shock of discovering who she really was had taken a toll. She wouldn't be able to sleep for hours. A walk might clear her head. She glanced at the sleeping baby. "I can't leave Christophe alone."

"Marie will stay with him. Tomorrow I will appoint more staff to take over his care, and yours."

Her chin came up. "I don't want my child cared for by staff, even if he is a prince. I prefer to look after him myself."

"You may not find it so easy to do everything yourself, now you are part of the royal household."

"I may be staying in one for the moment, but as for living here…"

He held up a restraining hand. "Tomorrow is soon enough to plan your future. Let's walk first."

Icy fingers caressed her spine. The prince's attitude reminded her uncomfortably of her adoptive father who invariably thought he knew what was best for her. "I do have some say in this," she reminded Josquin.

His dark eyebrows tilted upward. "Of course you do."

As long as her wishes coincided with his plans for her, she read into his silence. The walls of the château seemed confining suddenly. She had a few words with Marie about Christophe, then followed Josquin outside.

"What would you have done if I hadn't come to Carramer voluntarily?" she asked.

"With Prince Henry so ill, I would have found some other way to bring you home."

"Kidnap us, you mean?"

"It might have been…instructive."

Her temper flared. "Over my dead body. I may be a princess by birth, but I wasn't brought up to be compliant. You'd have had more of a fight on your hands than you bargained for."

A smile ghosted over his features. "You have more in common with your forebears than you realize. Members of the royal family—both my own and the Valmonts—are not known for their compliance."

She felt unwillingly warmed to think she might share family traits with them. "If you're typical of your family, you're hardly what I expected from royalty."

He led the way through a walled garden and out into

a larger, parklike area dotted with ancient trees and winding pathways that invited exploration. She could smell the sea, and a tantalizing ginger scent on the light breeze, and drew a deep breath.

"What did you expect?" he asked mildly.

"More reserve, stuffiness. Lots of pomp and ceremony." She tried to imagine him wearing a uniform straight out of *The Student Prince*. She found it surprisingly easy. He would look breathtaking, she imagined.

"We have our share of ceremony when required," he told her. "Prince Henry is more old-fashioned than I am."

"When will I meet him?" Her voice said she wasn't sure she wanted to.

"When his doctor advises he's up to it." He stopped in the shade of an ironwood tree and rested his hands on her shoulders. "Don't be concerned about the meeting. I've arranged to accompany you."

"I'm not concerned about it. Henry doesn't own me or Christophe." But she *was* troubled by Josquin's light touch on her shoulders. He stood closer than he had any business doing, and this time she didn't feel inclined to order him to move. Even if he would. He had only agreed last time because it suited him, she sensed, sure that Josquin didn't take orders easily. He acted more like a man used to giving them.

The garden was so quiet that Josquin heard the breath tighten in Sarah's throat. He waited for her to tell him to back off again. When she didn't, he kept his hands where they were and feasted his eyes on her beauty. He had dreamed of being close to her since seeing her photograph.

Finding that she came neatly up to his chin confirmed what he had long suspected. The photos hadn't done her

loveliness full justice. She had the classic de Valmont
bone structure: high cheekbones in a heart-shaped face,
complemented by the healthy glow of her American coloring. Her dark chestnut hair was so lustrous that it
gleamed like satin as it hung in a heavy curtain around
her nape. He was glad she hadn't had it curled artifi-
cially. Everything about her looked, felt, *smelled* won-
derfully natural.

Tempted to experiment, he slid one hand under her
hair, letting a few strands slide through his fingers. As
he cupped her nape, he heard another indrawn breath,
but still no objection. The tip of her tongue darted out
to moisten her full lips, and he almost kissed her there
and then, barely stopping himself in time.

The fascination he had experienced at seeing her photographs was nothing compared to the desire threatening
to consume him as she stood before him in the flesh. He
needed every ounce of discipline he possessed to step
away from her, aware that when she found out what he'd
done to her, she'd rather kill him than kiss him. The
thought was surprisingly disturbing.

Her composure looked fragile, he noted. Despite his
claim of a connection between them, he wished he could
be sure that she felt as drawn to him as he did to her. If
she did, he hardly let himself think what it could mean
or where it might lead. It couldn't be allowed to lead
anywhere.

"Why didn't you identify Christophe's father on his
papers?" he asked, deliberately refocussing his thoughts.

"Didn't your spies tell you everything?" she asked
tautly, horrified to think he had probably questioned her
friends, local business people, the art gallery staff, who
else? "My neighbors in North Hollywood must have

told them I'm a Jezebel with a child and no sign of a father.''

He kept his tone carefully neutral. ''Many women choose to bear children alone nowadays, even in Carramer.''

She let out a breath that ended on a shudder. ''Thank you.''

''For what?''

''For not judging me. Christophe's father...''

Josquin made himself wait although he burned with impatience to know everything about her, the living details, rather than the dry facts in a report. He also recognized something else, a gnawing jealousy of the man who had given her a child. What sort of man would do that, then refuse to accept the responsibility?

He soon found out.

''I've known Christophe's father all my life. He never wanted to be anything but a priest. If he knew he had fathered a baby, he would have given up his dream for us, and I couldn't let him sacrifice everything just because we'd let ourselves get carried away once.''

''So you didn't tell him.'' Josquin felt awed by the strength of spirit she must have needed to live with such a decision. At the same time, anger flared soul-deep inside him. If he'd been the man, he would have wanted to know about his child, regardless of the price to be paid.

She saw his jaw tighten. ''You don't agree with my decision?''

''I wasn't involved.'' But his hands tightened into fists at his sides.

She saw that, too. ''Maybe I was afraid it would come between us later, when he understood what he'd given

up. I want more for Christophe than parents who stay
together out of convenience.''

''Are you speaking of your adoptive parents?''

She nodded, moved by his perceptiveness. ''I don't
think Rose agreed with James's decision to adopt me
illegally. I had no idea what had happened, but I was
always aware of tension between them, and somehow I
knew it involved me. When they weren't arguing, they
ignored one another in frigid silence. I'm not sure which
was worse.''

''You had no say in your fate.''

She toyed with a low-hanging branch. ''I know that
now, but it didn't help while I was growing up. I don't
want my child ever to feel like that.''

''All the more reason to accept his heritage. He will
know who he is and where he belongs.''

She sighed. ''I will, given time. Learning that you're
a princess and your son is the heir to a throne is a lot
to take in.''

He noted she was no longer talking about leaving.
Good. He decided to be content with the small victory.
Later when she found out the rest, perhaps she would
accept that he had acted for her good.

''You're right, it is a lot to take in. We'll return to
the château and you should rest,'' he said.

''If I can.'' Her tone said she doubted it.

''I could have Henry's doctor stop by and give you
something.''

''Thank you. I'll be fine.''

Her nearness sent flares of need surging through him
until he almost threw caution to the wind and took her
into his arms. He knew it was ridiculous to feel so
strongly about a woman he had only known through reports and photographs until now, but he couldn't shake

the feeling that he already knew everything he needed to about her.

She was warm, passionate and strong enough to decide to raise her child alone, rather than risk a loveless marriage. She was also the most beautiful creature he had set eyes on. She made him want to do something he'd never done in his life, wish that he was other than he was.

He gave his head a slight shake, determinedly shrugging off the longing that gripped him. When she knew the truth, she was unlikely to give him the time of day, far less her love. He may as well accept the fact now, before he found himself in over his head.

He hoped it wasn't already too late.

"I think I could get used to royal life," Sarah said as Marie removed the breakfast tray from her knees. "You're spoiling me."

The attendant's eyes twinkled. "It's my job to spoil you, Your Highness."

"We've already been over this highness business. My friends call me Sarah, and I'd like you to do so when we're alone."

"As you wish, Your Highness. Shall I bring the little prince to you now?"

Sarah nodded. She could hardly believe this was happening to her. Yesterday she had been plain Sarah McInnes, unemployed gallery curator and single mother. Today she was a princess of Valmont, at least according to Josquin de Marigny.

She hadn't fully believed him until last night when he showed her photographs of Philippe, her birth father. Christophe was the spitting image of his grandfather, at the same age. Her strong resemblance to Prince Henry was also shocking. She didn't welcome the resemblance to her grandfather, but couldn't deny it.

His grandfather. Her father. She let the words roll around in her mind. They called forth a feeling of belonging she had almost despaired of knowing. To think she was a part of this most exquisite of kingdoms, was almost too much to take in. She may not approve of Josquin's tactic in bringing her to Carramer, but she couldn't fault the outcome.

Thinking of him, she felt an unaccustomed warmth spreading through her. As adviser to the ruler of the province, Josquin must have a million royal duties, yet he had devoted hours of his time to her yesterday. As Prince Henry's heir, Christophe was Josquin's main concern, but he hadn't seemed to mind spending time with her.

The feeling was far too mutual, she thought, frowning. If Josquin kept looking at her the way he had yesterday, as if he was sorely tempted to kiss her, she was going to have a hard time sticking to her vow of noninvolvement.

Impatient with this thought, she threw back the covers and pulled a robe over her nightgown. At least Christophe seemed happy in his new surroundings. Sarah couldn't remember the last time she had enjoyed an uninterrupted night's sleep.

She looked up as Marie came in with Christophe in her arms. "I was about to come and see to him. He hasn't slept this late for ages," Sarah said.

Marie smiled. "He awoke early so I bathed and changed him. He's hungry now and needs his mama."

This was going to take some getting used to, Sarah thought, pushing away a niggling feeling of guilt as Marie placed Christophe in her arms.

Sarah tickled him under his chubby chin. "How are you this morning, Your Highness?"

When he gooed and gurgled, clapping his hands, she buried her face in his soft body. "Full of beans as usual. Do you know how much I love you, baby of mine?"

Marie clasped her hands in front of her. "I think he knows."

Sarah had already learned that the other woman had a baby of her own, which explained why she was so good with Christophe. "How is your little one?" she asked.

Marie made a face. "Teething and complaining about it. My husband and I took turns getting up to him last night."

"Then what are you doing waiting on me? Go home to your baby."

"Who will take care of you and Prince Christophe?"

"We'll take care of ourselves. We've been doing it for a long time. Now go home or I'll have to pull royal rank on you." Not at all sure she could, she was pleased when Marie took the threat at face value.

"I'll send one of the other ladies-in-waiting along to make sure you're both all right," she promised.

"Very well," Sarah conceded good-humoredly. "But I don't want to see you back here until tomorrow, understood?"

Marie's smile broadened. "Who am I to argue with my princess?" She picked up the breakfast tray and left with something very like alacrity.

It felt good to be alone with Christophe, Sarah thought as she moved into the sitting room and settled him to feed. She was going to have trouble adjusting to having staff around her so much of the time. She might take Christophe out to explore the gardens, she thought, excited at the prospect. She didn't like to think part of the excitement might be at the prospect of running into Josquin in the grounds.

Thinking of him made her pause as she lifted the baby away. He began to fret until she settled him at her other breast where he suckled contentedly.

"Sorry, I got distracted," she told him apologetically. Josquin was enough to distract any woman, and she recognized that the attraction was far from one-sided. She wished she could shake off her suspicion that he wasn't telling her everything he knew.

The question nagged at her as she lifted Christophe against her shoulder and rubbed his back. "Prince Josquin acts like a man with a dangerous secret, don't you think?" she asked the baby. His response came in the form of a hearty burp.

She held the baby in front of her, smiling broadly at his contented expression. "Is that an opinion? Because I doubt if His Highness would appreciate it."

"What would His Highness not appreciate?"

She started as Josquin himself appeared in the doorway. Actually, loomed would be a more accurate term. He was so tall and broad-shouldered that he all but filled the opening. "Where I come from, it's customary to knock," she said, annoyed at the way her heart leaped at the sight of him.

"I rang for your attendant, but it seems you gave her the day off," he said, unperturbed by her rancor.

"I'm not used to having people fussing over me all the time."

He raised a dark eyebrow. "Surely you had servants in America?"

She had forgotten how much he knew about her. "We

had a housekeeper, but I would hardly call her a servant. She was part of the family.''

''As Marie and your other attendants are part of your family now.''

''Ah yes, that family.''

''You still sound unconvinced, although the resemblance between yourself and Prince Henry, and Christophe and your father is beyond dispute. May I?''

He stepped closer, holding out his arms. With a reluctance she could barely explain to herself, she gave the baby to him. To her surprise, Christophe seemed intrigued at finding himself in male arms, and began to play with the pewter pin adorning Josquin's tie. The prince looked pleased. ''I think he likes me.''

Since she couldn't explain her feelings to herself, she masked how much his comment bothered her. ''Christophe likes everyone. He's a real party animal.''

Over the baby's downy head, Josquin shot her a curious glance. ''Does he take after his mother?''

''I'm not a hermit, if that's what you mean. I take Christophe to playgroup, and we sometimes meet friends from the gallery where I used to work. But having a one-year-old baby doesn't do much for your social life.''

''I can imagine.'' He lifted the baby high into the air and brought him down, making an airplane noise as he did so. Christophe gurgled in delight and waved his chubby hands.

She watched, grudging the baby's evident enjoyment and reluctantly recognizing the symptoms of jealousy. ''For a bachelor, you're pretty good at that stuff.''

''My cousins' babies provide me with plenty of practice. They're going to love having Christophe as a playmate.''

Some demon drove her to say, "If we stay in Carramer long enough to meet them."

Josquin paused in the act of swinging Christophe into the air. "I thought you understood that this is your home."

"My father came from Valmont, but that doesn't make it home yet. You said we can leave anytime I want to, right?"

He hesitated for a heartbeat before nodding. "Now you know about your background, I hope you will want to stay in Carramer."

"I need more time to think this through."

Josquin frowned. "You may not have much time. Prince Henry's doctor says he's well enough to see you this morning."

Her heart turned over. She didn't know why the thought of meeting the old prince scared her, but it did. She stood up and took Christophe from Josquin's arms, holding the baby protectively against her. But protecting him from what? She didn't know. "When does Prince Henry want to see me?"

"As soon as you're dressed. I'll send someone to look after Christophe while you get ready."

"No, thanks. We'll be fine." She was already regretting sending Marie away, but it was too late now. She told herself she was used to dressing herself and taking care of Christophe at the same time. The only difference now was the setting. And the meeting ahead of them.

Josquin inclined his head. "Very well. I will send a lady-in-waiting to sit with the baby during your audience with Prince Henry. My equerry, Gerard, will escort you to the prince's chambers within an hour."

"I'll be ready," she agreed, but suspected that the opposite was true. How could she ever be ready to meet the royal tyrant who had destroyed her real parents' chance at happiness?

Chapter Four

At her first sight of Prince Henry, confusion churned through Sarah. She had braced herself to deal with a stubborn, elderly dictator in poor health. Propped up on a chaise and surrounded by cushions, he appeared surprisingly robust.

Deep of chest and broad of shoulder, Prince Henry had a lion's mane of silver hair and aristocratic features frozen in a disdainful expression. To Sarah's uncertain gaze, he looked regal and terrifying. She lifted her chin, determined not to let him see how intimidated she was.

Did impressive looks run in all royal families? she wondered with a quick glance at Josquin.

"Don't be deceived by appearances," he murmured into her ear. "Henry is much frailer than he looks."

Belatedly she noticed the mask dangling from the arm of Henry's chair, leading to an oxygen tank set up behind his chair. She hardened her heart against the wave of sympathy that threatened to undermine her self-possession. Prince Henry didn't deserve her compassion.

She had made up her mind not to curtsy. Her American half rebelled against it. She wasn't sure yet what her princess half wanted to do. That was still too new. So she walked toward Prince Henry with her head high, Josquin's presence at her side bolstering her courage.

"Your Highness, may I present Princess Sarina de Valmont."

Henry's black-eyed gaze raked her before swinging to Josquin. "You may. But where is my heir?"

No welcome? No admission that Sarah was his estranged granddaughter? Two could play that game. "With his nanny, Your Highness," she said coldly, not waiting for Josquin to speak for her. "And I prefer to be known as Sarah."

"Do you now?" Prince Henry gestured to Josquin. "Bring the child to me."

Josquin started to move but she was faster, forestalling him with a hand on his arm. "In a few minutes."

Prince Henry's head shot up and his eyes flashed fire. "What did you say?"

"You and I need to talk first, Your Highness—Grandfather." She used the titles with cool precision, as she might have aimed a weapon. Before he got anywhere near her son, the old prince was going to acknowledge their relationship first.

Out of the corner of her eye, she saw Josquin fighting not to smile. What did he find so amusing? she wondered angrily. Prince Henry may be the ruler of Valmont Province under an ancient charter granted by the monarch of Carramer, but he was also the man who had destroyed her real family.

To her amazement, the old prince gave a gravelly chuckle and his sharp-eyed gaze went to Josquin. "She's a de Valmont, all right."

Josquin nodded, his eyes dancing. "I warned you, Henry."

She felt a frown settle over her eyes. Had Josquin smiled because he knew her attitude was the only one Prince Henry would respect? Josquin might have forewarned her. She felt as if she and Christophe were on one side of a battle line, with Josquin and his uncle on the other.

"I'm glad the two of you find my situation amusing." She let the ice in her voice warn them that she didn't.

Josquin looked as if he didn't like being arraigned beside his uncle. Surely he didn't expect her to think he was on her side?

"I wasn't laughing at you, girl," Prince Henry said. "Believe me, I've had years enough to regret that you weren't brought up here where you belong."

"Then I wouldn't have had Christophe," she reminded him.

Did she imagine a momentary softening in Prince Henry's gaze? He frowned, dispelling any such impression. "You may have had an heir of pure Carramer blood instead."

Pure or not, she felt her blood start to boil. "Then let us return to America, and I won't sully your family with our tainted bloodlines any longer."

"As Josquin has no doubt informed you, I may not have the luxury of time or choice. Valmont is ruled by my family only so long as there is a male heir."

She shot Josquin a shocked glance. He hadn't told her any such thing. Too busy looking at her with those bedroom eyes, she thought, trying to be furious and barely succeeding. Was Josquin really attracted to her, or was his attention only an act to make her want to remain in Carramer?

"From what Josquin tells me, your bloodlines are anything but tainted," the old prince continued. "Your mother's family can be traced back to a minor branch of the British royal family."

She quashed the thrill that ran through her, annoyed at learning more about her mother secondhand. What other surprises lay in store for her? "Josquin hasn't seen fit to tell me much of anything yet," she said, skewering him with an angry look.

"Typical, typical," Henry muttered to Josquin. "Wants everything in the first twenty-four hours she's here. Don't they teach you patience in America?"

"As an American, I learned all I needed to know, starting with the fact that everyone is created equal."

"The same holds true in Carramer," Josquin observed, his expression telling her he was enjoying the interplay between grandfather and granddaughter.

Well, that made one of them. Sarah's gesture encompassed the lavishly furnished room, the portraits of generations of de Valmonts and de Marignys, the antique furnishings and Persian carpets. "We have different definitions of equality. In America, we don't live in palaces, and we don't curtsy to anyone."

"It isn't a requirement here," Josquin assured her.

"Just as well, since you'd obviously have a hard time bending your knee to anybody," Prince Henry growled. "For goodness' sake sit down. I'm getting a sore neck staring up at the pair of you."

The only chair close to Henry's was a velvet upholstered love seat, and she perched on the edge of it gingerly, trying to keep some space between herself and Josquin as he sat down beside her. Trying to keep her wits about her was enough of a challenge, without the distraction of his hard body pressing against hers.

She told herself he was only using her to please Prince Henry. Any attraction was on her side alone. The thought notched her tension higher. Far from seeing him as attractive, she was having difficulty remembering that he was the reason she was in this predicament.

He sat as close to her as she'd feared, but didn't seem to find it a problem. Completely relaxed, he stretched an arm along the back of the seat, the sleeve of his suit brushing her nape. A hint of pine fragrance slid over her, fogging her senses.

He hooked one leg over the other at the knee and she became mesmerized by the pattern on the sole of his highly polished shoe. A black sock hugged his narrow ankle, disappearing beneath a cylinder of impeccably tailored fabric. Her gaze had slid all the way along his raised leg before she stopped, her pulse racing. The urge to follow the path of her gaze with her hand was almost irresistible.

She forgot where she was, why she was here until Christophe's dear, baby face rose before her eyes. She jerked her gaze back to Prince Henry, horrified at letting herself be sidetracked by Josquin's sheer physicality even for a moment.

Did she have a choice? Something about him compelled her attention every time he shared the same space with her. If she wasn't careful he would make her forget all the reasons she had to mistrust him. Even if she was careful, she feared. All the more reason to harden her heart against his appeal.

He was in control and she wasn't, she ticked off mentally. He had been born a prince. She hadn't. She would never get used to being called Princess Sarina. The thought that she might want to sent another chill frosting down her spine.

"Are you telling me that Carramer citizens don't have to bow to royalty, Prince Henry?" she asked, irritated at the tremor she heard in her voice.

Henry shook his head. "They choose to do so, out of respect for everything the monarchy does for the country."

Josquin turned to her, the slight contact firing a thousand volts of awareness along her nerves, although she tried to prevent it. Might as well try to stop the sun from shining.

"Over the centuries, our people have had several opportunities to vote against retaining the royal family," he said.

"And we're still here," Henry observed. "So you can stop imagining us as some antiquated boot crushing the people of Carramer under our heel."

She had been trying to cast Henry in that light, she realized. Easier than dealing with him as a person. More like herself than she wanted him to be, if genetics were anything to go by. "What do you want from me?" she asked wearily.

"Only what your birthright obligates you to do," Henry said.

She stood up, bracing her hands on her hips, wondering if she was confronting Henry or putting some distance between herself and Josquin. "Isn't it a little late to remind me of my birthright and my obligations, Prince Henry?"

Henry's frown deepened. "We can't change history."

But he could acknowledge the wrongs he had done to her family, she thought. She had never disliked anyone as much as she did the stubborn old prince, and by extension his royal yes man, she thought.

With an inner sigh, she conceded that Josquin was

anything but a yes man. In Henry's presence, she had seen no sign that Josquin was anything but his own man, and she suspected Henry appreciated Josquin's independent spirit. The old prince probably had plenty of lackeys currying his favor. From Josquin he would get honest opinions, disagreement when warranted and an enviable loyalty. She had already seen enough of Josquin to be sure that her assessment was accurate.

She didn't want to be impressed by Josquin, but he was the kind of man who left her no choice. Careful, she cautioned herself, hoping the warning wasn't already too late. Josquin was an obstacle to getting Christophe away from Carramer. Liking him was a bad idea. Anything more than liking was unthinkable.

He stood up beside her. "Sarah's had a lot to take in over the past twenty-four hours, Henry. We should give her more time."

"We'd all like more time," Henry growled. "In my state of health, I can't afford to wait too long, before burdening her with royal duties."

"Royal duties?" she said, shooting a savage look at Josquin. "Evidently Prince Josquin hasn't acquainted you with the circumstances of my arrival in Carramer, Your Highness. I was lured here under completely false pretenses. I'm neither prepared, nor willing, to undertake a royal role."

"I note you don't dispute your heritage," Henry said dryly.

"Josquin has shown me enough photos of my…my birth father…to convince me that this isn't a colossal mistake," she said. And facing the man before her was uncomfortably like looking into a mirror a couple of generations apart. "However, an accident of birth doesn't make me a princess, any more than it makes my child your heir.''

''That's where you're wrong,'' Josquin said quietly, the steel in his voice warning her that she had gone too far.

She didn't care. Throwing caution to the wind, she swung around. ''You can't force us to stay and do your bidding.''

Josquin's expression was unreadable. ''While on Carramer soil, you are subject to Carramer law.''

''Then we'll remove ourselves from Carramer.''

''I forbid any such thing.'' Henry's voice rang with royal command. ''You must…''

Whatever else he wanted to say lost in a fit of coughing. Moving to his uncle's side, Josquin pressed a button set into Henry's chair. A uniformed nurse rushed in and adjusted the cylinder behind the prince's chair. Henry's chest heaved as he drew in the life-giving oxygen. Above the mask, his eyes burned with anger.

Sarah felt at a loss. It was hard to hate someone who was obviously suffering, but she couldn't allow her baby to become the pawn of a man with as few scruples as Prince Henry. ''I don't mean to cause you distress, Your Highness,'' she said evenly. ''But I mean what I say. I intend to leave Carramer right away, and take my baby with me.''

To the obvious concern of his nurse, Henry wrenched the mask of his face. ''Tell her,'' he ordered Josquin.

She looked uncertainly at Josquin. ''Tell me what?''

Josquin took her arm none too gently. ''Not here. Henry needs to rest.''

What about what she needed? ''I insist on knowing what you want from me.''

Josquin swung away from her, her refusal to cooperate

and lack of consideration for Prince Henry, fueling the prince's obvious anger. She was slightly appalled at her own behavior, but was too overwrought to moderate it.

"We don't want anything from you," Josquin said in tone like breaking glass. "Your task was done when you brought Christophe back to Valmont."

"You mean you would keep him here with or without me?" She could hardly force the words out. She had wanted honesty. She could hardly blame Josquin for giving it to her. But the ground felt as if it could give way beneath her feet at any second. "You can't. We have rights."

Josquin's expression was implacable. "Your duty as a princess comes before personal considerations."

"Even if it costs me my son?"

"There's no need to be melodramatic. Your son is where he belongs."

"He belongs with his mother."

"Then the solution is obvious."

She saw the trap even as Josquin sprang it closed. She had two choices: remain in Carramer with her precious baby, or return to America without him. Not two choices, only one, she thought with a sinking heart.

"I seem to have no option but to stay for the time being," she said, edging her voice with ice. "But I will never accept being a part of a family that treats its members so brutally."

Prince Henry coughed. "Whether you accept the situation or not, doesn't alter the fact that your son is my heir." He waved away the nurse trying to fuss over him, and summoned some reserve of determination. "I won't let Valmont be sacrificed to your stubbornness."

She pushed at her hair. "I don't understand."

Henry glared at Josquin. "Make her understand. Take

her away and teach her what she needs to know to behave like a princess of Carramer.''

''But I don't...''

''Enough.'' None too gently, Josquin took her arm and steered her toward the door.

She looked back to see the nurse replacing the mask over Prince Henry's face. The old prince's eyes glittered with anger and frustration. She shivered at the thought of her child's future being in the hands of such a heartless man.

Chapter Five

Josquin's pace didn't slacken until they reached her suite. His thunderous expression startled the lady-in-waiting who was watching Christophe, but the woman was too well trained to react to his curt thanks and dismissal. She curtsied and left.

Sarah wished that she could snatch up Christophe and do the same, without the curtsy. But the baby looked so happy in his playpen in the center of the sitting room, piling soft alphabet blocks on top of one another and laughing when they tumbled over, that she couldn't bear to upset him.

"What did Prince Henry mean by 'make her understand'?" she demanded.

Josquin's breath hissed out. "You don't give up, do you? Henry can barely take a breath without suffering, yet you won't be happy until you provoke him to the point of collapse."

She hadn't liked her behavior toward the old prince any more than Josquin did. Was it possible that she was more like her grandfather than she wanted to accept? "I'm sorry," she said, unnerved by the idea. "He looked well enough. Until he had trouble breathing, I didn't realize how ill he is."

"His condition deteriorates if he becomes overly stressed," Josquin told her shortly. "Which unfortunately leaves the future of this province in your hands. And mine, since Henry entrusted me with your royal tutelage."

He didn't sound pleased about it, she thought uncomfortably. When had she started caring what he thought of her?

"You know the old saying about leading a horse to water?" she said with a lightness that didn't quite come off. In truth she was ashamed of her behavior toward Prince Henry. No matter what the provocation, she should have shown more consideration for him.

"In Carramer, we have a different saying: 'the horse that refuses water refuses life.'"

She pursed her lips, looking down at her child. "The life you expect Christophe and me to live doesn't hold much appeal." She had had enough of having her life controlled by a man who thought he knew what was best for her. She wasn't about to let Prince Henry take over where James had left off.

"Isn't it time you stopped worrying about what you want, and started thinking of your son?"

"I *am* thinking of Christophe." Her arms ached to pick him up. In her present state, she was afraid she might drop him. "He doesn't deserve to be a pawn in your game."

Josquin's gaze went to the baby. One of the blocks had tumbled out of his reach, and Josquin leaned into the pen to give it back to him. Christophe took it, smiling. If only he knew, he was smiling at the devil, she thought.

Josquin straightened. "Is that how you see this? As a game?"

She recoiled from his arctic tone. "Not a game exactly. But you must agree that you and Prince Henry manipulate people to suit your own ends?"

He broke off as the lady-in-waiting returned with a laden tray that she placed on a side table. "We'll serve ourselves, thank you," Josquin told her.

The woman looked uncertainly from Josquin to Sarah, and back to the prince again, "Will there be anything else?"

"No, thank you."

On a sudden whim, Sarah smiled at the woman. "What is your name?"

At the door, the woman turned, "Perin Collier, Your Highness."

"Thank you for taking care of Christophe this morning, Perin."

Perin's pretty face lightened. "My pleasure, madam. He's a delightful baby."

"That will be all…Perin."

Did Sarah imagine it, or did Josquin emphasize the woman's name? As Perin left, Sarah suppressed a smile. She wasn't the only one with a few things to learn. Her mood lifted at the thought, then crashed again as Josquin gestured peremptorily toward the tray. Princes were above serving themselves coffee, she gathered.

They had more important things to argue about, so she went to the tray and poured two cups of coffee from a heavy silver pot into porcelain cups that were so fine, they were almost translucent. The simple act reminded her of her American grandmother, who had used and loved such fine things. A wave of homesickness rolled over her and she swayed slightly.

"Is something the matter?" Josquin asked sharply, moving to her side.

She forced the weakness away and squared her shoulders. "A touch of jet lag, most likely. Cream? Sugar?"

"Black, thank you."

She handed him the cup. When she offered him a plate of petit fours, he gestured a refusal. She wasn't hungry, either, but chose a plain finger of shortbread for Christophe to chew on. The baby's chubby fingers closed around the treat, and he pushed it into his mouth enthusiastically. How uncomplicated his life was, she thought with a touch of envy. She suppressed a shudder, promising herself that his life would stay uncomplicated, no matter what the cost to herself.

She swung back to Josquin, holding her cup between them like a shield. "You were saying?"

His frown returned. "No one is being manipulated. There is more at stake here than you know."

"Then tell me what it is."

"The future of Valmont Province."

She hadn't expected him to credit her with so much importance. She took a sip of coffee, almost choking as the scalding liquid seared her throat. "You mean because of this charter business?"

He nodded. "Under the charter, if Henry has no male heir, the province returns to Carramer rule."

"Your cousin, Prince Lorne, takes over," she said, thinking out loud, and saw Josquin nod. "Is he such a tyrant that the people of Valmont would suffer under his rule?"

Josquin's mouth twitched, the first sign of any real softening toward her she'd seen in hours. She was surprised at how much her spirits lifted. "Lorne would be horrified to hear himself described as a tyrant. He is one of the most benign rulers Carramer has known."

She took another, more cautious sip of coffee, and set the cup down. "Then what's the problem?"

"The problem, as you call it, is that Valmont has its own history. Centuries of tradition are not to be discarded lightly. You are a de Valmont yourself. If you were instrumental in letting the charter lapse, you would be throwing away your own history, and your son's birthright."

Something tugged at her. She hated to accept that Josquin might be right. She might be a de Valmont by birth, but she was American in every way that mattered. So why did she feel so troubled by Josquin's statement?

She began to pace, aware of Christophe following her with his eyes. "This is crazy," she said, as much for herself as for the prince. "A couple of weeks ago, we barely knew there was any such place as Valmont. You can't expect us to give up the only life we know because of some heritage that means nothing to Christophe and me."

The note of appeal in her tone made Josquin arch his brow. "I suspect your heritage means more to you than you want to accept."

When had he begun to read her so accurately? She stopped pacing and spread her hands. "How can you be so sure?" Especially when she wasn't.

He replaced his cup on the tray, and came closer. "Because of who you are, and who your son is."

He had such compelling eyes, she thought, annoyed at the distraction. "Damn it, don't read my mind."

"I don't have to," he said, his voice deepening. "I

can see the truth in your eyes. You want Valmont for your child.''

''Perhaps.'' Her own voice dropped almost to a whisper. Josquin was right. She had lain awake far into last night, thinking about Christophe and the life he would have as heir to the throne of Valmont. What could she possibly offer him that could compare with hundreds of years of history?

She knew she wasn't thinking only of the material benefits, although goodness knew, he would have far more here than she could provide for him in a walk-up apartment in North Hollywood. More importantly he would know who he was, and who his forebears were, all the way back to the creation of these lovely islands.

Her eyes brimmed as she looked at the baby. Not for him, the desolation she'd suffered after finding out she was adopted. Christophe would know as much about his birth father as she could tell him. And as a prince of Carramer, he would never wonder who he was, or where he came from, as she'd done during the last two agonizing years.

''Yes,'' she said on an outrush of breath.

Josquin was gracious in victory. ''You have made the right decision.''

''I haven't made it yet.''

His gaze went from her to the baby and back. ''You may not think so, but you have.''

She felt her temper rise. ''Do princes always expect to get their own way?''

''Most men do, whether they are princes or not,'' he observed. ''Although in my experience, a smart woman makes sure a man gets her own way.''

''Another old Carramer saying?''

''A statement of fact.'' He reached into the playpen

and lifted Christophe out. The baby laughed in delight, smearing soggy shortbread on the prince's lapel. Josquin didn't seem to notice. She was torn between the urge to snatch the child back, and admiration at the assured way Josquin handled the baby.

"You don't look very regal at this moment, my young friend," he told Christophe. "But you do look happy."

The note of yearning she heard in Josquin's voice made her pause. "You sound as if you envy my son."

"Why not? He has so much."

"Compared to you, he has had very little."

Josquin's bleak gaze seared her. "He is healthy, protected, loved beyond measure. He has a mother who puts his well being above her own needs."

The way Josquin put it, her son was indeed blessed, she thought, feeling an unaccustomed swell of pride. Why had she focused only on what she couldn't give Christophe, without considering how much she *had* given him. "Surely you had all those things and more?" she asked, hearing herself sounding choked.

She watched his expression change to cool and aloof. "You'd be surprised."

A chill seeped through her, but for him rather than herself. What wasn't he telling her? "Your parents didn't love you?"

"On the contrary. They loved me very much."

Past tense? "What happened?"

"My father died seven years ago."

"I'm sorry," she said softly.

The prince inclined his head, blowing gently on Christophe's silky hair to ruffle it. The baby pawed Josquin's mouth and he closed it gently around the tiny fingers, and Sarah felt a pang imagining the prince's lips against her own.

"What about your mother?" she asked, dry-mouthed.

He untangled the baby's fingers and retrieved another biscuit, which he handed to Christophe. Distracted, the baby started gnawing on it. "My mother, Princess Fleur, lives on a family estate near Solano, the capital of Carramer," he explained. "She has her life and I have mine."

From his tone, she gathered that he and his mother weren't close. She considered what little she knew about royal life. "Were you raised by tutors and nannies?"

"We couldn't afford them, at least not for long," he surprised her by saying. "My mother was somewhat—profligate—with our resources."

His mother spent money like water, she translated. Insight flashed through her. "That's how Prince Henry became your mentor isn't it, and why you feel so obligated to him?"

"Appreciative might be a better word than obligated. When my parents neglected their responsibility toward me, Henry took over my education and provided me with opportunities I wouldn't otherwise have had."

She nodded her understanding. "I may not be able to forgive my adoptive parents for what they did to me, but they gave me a good education and a comfortable lifestyle." More than Josquin had received from his parents, from the sound of things. His loyalty to the old prince started to make sense.

Compassion for Josquin stirred deep inside, startling her. His cool aloofness wasn't directed at her. His upbringing had created him, as much as her American background had created her. Neither of them could help being the way they were. The chemistry she had felt vibrating between them from first meeting notched higher in intensity.

She had taken two steps toward him when another thought occurred to her, freezing her in place. "One thing you haven't mentioned is who rules Valmont while Christophe is still a child?"

Josquin tensed, as if sensing the question was important to her, to them. It was, but possibly not in the way he might imagine. "Naturally Prince Henry does," he told her.

"You said that Prince Henry's illness may make that impossible for much longer." She felt the compassion, the yearning drain away, replaced by a soul-deep anger she could barely put into words. "This isn't about Christophe at all, is it?"

He jiggled the baby on his hip, not looking at her. "Your mother isn't making much sense, little one."

"I'm making plenty of sense, finally. I see now why you're so anxious to see Christophe installed as Henry's heir. If anything happens to Prince Henry, because Christophe is only a baby, it means you'll be the one ruling in Christophe's place, won't you? I imagine becoming Crown Regent of Valmont would solve a lot of your financial problems."

She practically snatched her child from Josquin's arms. He didn't resist. Why should he? They weren't going anywhere. Her adoptive father's favorite saying came back to her. "When someone wants to do you a favor, look for what they have to gain."

Josquin had a throne to gain. And Christophe was his passport.

Chapter Six

How could she have believed Josquin when he talked about the attraction between them? she berated herself as she lay in the deep claw-footed bath, trying to dull her senses with the heat of the water and the perfume of wild orchid bath oil. She felt too angry for either to do her much good.

She had wanted to believe him. Her own yearning to belong somewhere, be loved by someone, was more powerful than she had suspected. Josquin had found her weakness, then exploited her vulnerability for his own benefit. She couldn't believe how much that hurt.

She had waited for him to deny her accusation that he wanted to install Christophe as Henry's heir, so he could take over as Crown Regent in time. She was almost relieved when he said nothing. She wouldn't have believed his denial anyway. He didn't know her, so how could he feel anything for her, as he said?

She might have known he would have his own

agenda, just as her adoptive parents had had theirs. She
may as well accept that she was on her own—again.

She had been at Château de Valmont for two weeks,
and her education as a princess was rapidly taking shape.
Since she could do nothing else for the time being, she
had decided to cooperate, studying the Carramer language, history and customs with the succession of tutors
Josquin engaged. In her studies, there had to be something she could use to get herself and Christophe away
from Carramer.

Nothing so far had given her an idea. She could in-
troduce herself and comment on weather in Carramer.
She could manage a passable curtsy, and knew the difference between a baron and a baronet.

She could also recognize palace security from twenty
paces away. Male or female, military or civilian, they
had a way of making their presence felt. Not used to
having someone watch her every minute, she was aware
of minders hovering at a discreet distance, whenever she
ventured into the grounds of the château.

Protection or guard? She didn't know, and didn't care.
She had to believe that an opportunity to escape would
show itself. In the meantime, she would be a good student and learn how to behave like a princess. If she kept
it up long enough, Josquin might relax his vigilance long
enough for her to get Christophe away from him.

Christophe was thriving on the attention, she thought,
extending each leg in turn, and massaging fragrant oil
into her skin. Her ladies-in-waiting, Marie and Perin,
divided his care between them, all but squabbling over
who would take him to play on the beach, or entertain
him while Sarah was occupied. With Sarah's blessing,
Marie occasionally brought her own baby to the château
to play with Christophe. All the staff seemed positively

affronted when Sarah insisted on having time alone with Christophe every day.

She felt a surge of anger. Christophe was her baby. He might be the heir to the Valmont legacy, but he was still her child, not a pawn to help Josquin achieve his ambitions.

How far would Josquin have taken this supposed attraction between them, if she hadn't unmasked his real purpose? She told herself she didn't care, but heat seared through her every time he was nearby. She cursed herself for a fool, even as her body betrayed her with yearnings she didn't welcome, but couldn't seem to restrain. She wanted him, for all the good it would do her.

Angry with herself, she stood up, water streaming off her in fragrant rivulets, and reached for a bath sheet. Monogrammed of course. She swathed herself in it and wound another towel around her damp hair.

When she padded out Josquin was waiting in the sitting room.

She debated retreating to the bathroom, or trying for a dignified march past him to the bedroom, then decided to do neither. She took a steadying breath and confronted him as calmly if she were decently attired, ignoring the rapid pounding of her heart. "What are you doing here?"

Josquin was glad she couldn't see the effect she was having on him. Clad only in a couple of white towels, she managed to look defiantly regal. She didn't need lessons to turn her into a princess, he thought. The genes were manifest in the aristocratic shape of her features and her confident bearing—even when he would swear she didn't feel confident.

Had he been a romantic, he might have written a poem to her. With parents like his, he'd been forced to become a realist from an early age. Poetry and fantasies were luxuries he couldn't afford. He hadn't missed such things until Sarah came into his life.

When he was with her, his senses quickened and he longed to be able to put into words the feelings she aroused in him, not only physical—although they were powerful enough to take his breath away—but protective and nurturing. She threatened to free aspects of himself he'd never allowed to surface.

He breathed in the arousing fragrance surrounding her. Her skin glowed golden from her bath. He'd heard her splashing in the tub, and had fought a battle with himself not to go in.

He didn't have the right. She'd made her opinion of him clear when she found out that, should anything happen to Henry, Josquin would become Crown Regent until Christophe was of age. He told himself he welcomed her antagonism as a barrier between them. With his family fortunes in disarray, he couldn't afford romantic entanglements. Sarah was the first woman in a long time to make him wish that he could.

He steadied his voice with an effort. "Prince Henry is much better today. He's asking to see Christophe."

"Commanding his presence, don't you mean?"

"He asked." Josquin had been surprised, too. Ill health must be tempering Henry's usually autocratic manner. Or else Sarah herself was. Josquin hadn't missed the anxious way Henry had looked at his granddaughter, as if she might disappear if he said the wrong thing.

Sarah's inviting mouth tightened. "Should I be grateful he asked to see Christophe, instead of ordering us into his presence?"

"If you'd known him before he became ill, you wouldn't have to ask."

She was afraid, Josquin realized suddenly, seeing the turmoil in her lovely gray-green eyes, and the way her fingers tightened around the towel. He hated to think he was contributing to her fear.

"Henry means well," he said, wanting to allay her anxiety and not sure why. "All his life, he has placed the good of the country ahead of his own desires. Had he followed his heart, Philippe and your mother would have had his blessing."

"He put politics before his son's life," she snapped. "Am I supposed to forgive him, considering where it left me and *my* son?"

"Forgiving him would give both of you a new start, before it's too late."

"Are you saying I'm making the same mistake he did?"

"Only you know the answer to that. But I wish you'd give yourself the chance to get to know him, for Christophe's sake if not your own, especially considering the precarious state of Henry's health."

Was she supposed to pity the old prince now? To her amazement, Sarah found she did. Like it or not, Henry was her grandfather, her flesh and blood. Whatever mistakes he had made in the past paled beside that reality.

"I can try," she conceded on a heavy sigh. "Let's get this over with."

Josquin's mouth twitched. "Aren't you forgetting something?" His gesture indicated the towel wrapped around her.

Delicate color suffused her cheeks. "I'd better get dressed."

If she didn't, Josquin wouldn't answer for the consequences, he thought. She looked so sweet and utterly feminine that it was all he could do not to take her in his arms, although he was curious as to why he wanted to so badly.

Beautiful women weren't exactly rare at court. As a bachelor, Josquin was a popular target for society mothers wanting to aim their daughters at him, although he doubted they'd be so enthusiastic if they knew that all he had to offer for the moment was a title, and his position as Henry's protégé.

So why did he feel so drawn to Sarah? Her vulnerability appealed to him. Raised as his parents' go-between, he was used to soothing hurts and solving problems. Yet he didn't want to soothe Sarah. He wanted to drive her wild with passion, until her eyes flamed with desire for him, and her lithe body tangled with his in the dance of love.

Alarm bells rang in his head. He had no business imagining her in any way other than as Christophe's mother. Just as well he had allowed her to think ambition was his only motive for keeping her and her child in Carramer. He had seen the antagonism in her gaze when she found out.

She was wrong, but he couldn't afford to disillusion her. He needed her to hate him if he was to remain alone, as he must. The thought gave him little satisfaction.

The sounds of Sarah dressing reached him through the half-open door of her bedroom, and his imagination went into overdrive. His palms grew moist and he had to make an effort to unclench them. "Where is Christophe now?" he asked to drown out the provocative sounds.

Her bell-like voice floated through to him. "Perin took him for a walk. They should be back any minute."

He heard something slither to the floor. A bump and

mutter of annoyance as she retrieved whatever it was. Visions of the frivolous underwear women liked to wear danced through his head. Black lace? No, peach. Sarah had a soft core that he could picture swathed in peach.

Stop it, he ordered himself. Concentrate on the task at hand, reconciling her and her grandfather. Everything else could wait.

Now where had that thought come from? he asked himself uneasily. She blamed him for her predicament. That wasn't likely to change, no matter how many fortunes he recouped.

His breath caught as she emerged from the bedroom. Josquin had arranged for several court designers to bring a selection of clothes to the château for her to choose from. After arguing with him that her own clothes were sufficient, she had yielded to Josquin's logic that a holiday wardrobe hardly allowed for royal activities. Her present outfit showed she had chosen exquisitely.

She wore a long skirt of deepest blue, slit to the knee on each side, with a sheer, sea green blouse in a traditional Carramer design, fastened by a single pearl button over a dark camisole. The slinky material emphasized her slenderness, and the colors lent a sparkle to her glorious eyes.

"You look every inch a princess," he said on a harsh outpouring of breath.

"Are you going to take me?" she asked innocently.

Something twisted inside him. He wanted to more than she knew. "Perin will accompany you. I have an official commitment." His uneven tone betrayed how much he wished he hadn't.

Her long lashes veiled eyes he would swear held disappointment. "Far be it from me to keep you from your royal duties."

He heard the hint of panic in her tone. "You'll be fine. Henry is your grandfather, after all." He couldn't resist. "Besides, you don't need an escort who is arrogant, unscrupulous and power hungry."

Her fear was replaced by surprise, as he'd intended. "I didn't say you were any of those things."

"It was in your expression when you found out I could become Christophe's regent."

"Then I'll have to control what my eyes are saying."

She couldn't. Her eyes were like windows to her soul, revealing far more than she knew. "Are you telling me you don't think so badly of me?"

She twisted her hands together. "One minute you tell me you're attracted to me, the next I find I'm a stepping stone to your ambition. I don't know what to think."

"I have never lied to you directly, Sarah," he said quietly. "I admit I lured you to Carramer under false pretenses, but from the moment you arrived, I have been honest with you."

"In everything?" Her voice was a husky whisper.

"In everything."

Her eyes spoke again, in invitation this time. He stepped closer, knowing he was going to answer, knowing he shouldn't, but unable to stop himself if his life depended upon it. He kissed her.

At the first taste of her mouth, elemental awareness powered through him. He slid his hands around her shoulders, pulling her closer. After a tiny, almost imperceptible resistance, she sighed and relaxed against him as if she had dreamed of this as much as he had.

Control slid out of his hands into hers. He felt the moment it happened, and almost recoiled in shock. He was supposed to be kissing her. But as her pliant body shaped to his, and her lips moved provocatively under him, he knew this was as mutual as a kiss could ever be.

He had expected her to let him kiss her. He'd read the willingness in her eyes. But her eagerness astonished him. A tidal wave of sensations flooded through him. His whole being snapped and crackled, as needs he had long denied exploded along every nerve ending.

Heat radiated through Sarah as she kissed Josquin. His mouth and his body felt gloriously hard and masculine against her softness. She had told herself she would let him kiss her once, to see what it felt like. Now she knew, she was afraid that once would never be enough.

She took and took with her mouth until her limbs went weak, her heart raced, her palms grew damp. Still she took from him, and he answered her need with a generosity that left her breathless.

Words failed. Thoughts failed. For once she could only feel. Her heightened senses registered everything about him, from the slight abrasion of his closely shaved jaw against her newly bathed and oiled skin, to the heated press of his hands on her shoulders. His touch felt feverish, or maybe it was her own soaring temperature making her feel so hot.

He stepped away as if it cost him. It certainly cost her. She hadn't wanted the feeling to end. Now it had, she felt shaken, trembly. She looked away, lost for words.

He touched her chin, turning her to meet his intense gaze. She saw herself mirrored in his dark eyes as if in a glassy, stormy sea. "Sarina."

He said the Carramer version of her name like a caress. Moving as stiffly as a sleepwalker, she went to the window and braced her palms against the sill, gazing out to the ocean. Her home lay across that expanse of azure sea, but right now, America seemed as far away as the moon.

Here on Carramer, in this room, was a reality far more potent in its effect on her, she realized. Was that what Josquin wanted her to think? She spun around, fear lighting her gaze. "This won't work, Josquin."

He looked baffled. "What do you mean?"

She refused to let herself be fooled. "You're right about the chemistry between us. I felt it the moment we met, but I was a fool to give in to it, even for a second."

"At least you admit it was mutual. So how can you suspect a plot on my part?"

Her thoughts spun. "Fall in love with you, and I fall in love with Carramer. I accept Henry's plans for us, and you get the keys to the kingdom."

"Is that why you think I kissed you, to make you want to stay?"

"What else am I supposed to think? Do you care about me? Were you thinking commitment when you kissed me?"

He shook his head. "Marriage is out of the question for me."

She hadn't mentioned marriage, so why did she feel so shattered, since she didn't want any such thing from Josquin?

His message was clear. To him, the kiss was a means to an end. To her, it was...what? Not love, she rejected the thought outright. She didn't want to love Josquin. She wanted to get herself and her child as far away from him as she could. "At least you're honest," she said.

"You deserve no less."

"That's the first sentiment we fully agree on," she muttered. "I'd better finish getting ready. Perin should be back any minute with Christophe."

By then, she hoped, she would have banished her feelings of arousal to a place where they couldn't eat her up with longings she had no business feeling. She had to reapply her eye makeup three times because her hand was shaking so badly. She was unaware that her senses were straining to hear Josquin in the next room, until the sound of the outer door closing told her he was gone.

Chapter Seven

"As usual, it's just you and me, Chris," she told the baby in her arms, resisting the urge to feel sorry for herself. She was the one who had allowed Josquin to kiss her. She could hardly blame him for how much she had enjoyed it. He may well have been trying to seduce her so she would want to remain in Carramer, but her response was her own.

Christophe glowed from his careful exposure to the Carramer sun and crystalline fresh air. After feeding and changing him, she'd dressed him in a new white shirt and pants in a happy striped fabric. On his feet he wore tiny red leather shoes to match the pants. He looked adorable.

"You always look adorable," she said, swinging him high into her arms, and trying not to resent the royal family for being able to provide more for Chris than she could alone. The clothes were only part of their bounty. Within a few days of their arrival at Château de Valmont, everything a one-year-old could possibly need had been delivered to the palace.

Not for a prince, the secondhand crib and changing table she'd painted in a cheerful lemon color in her apartment back home, although Christophe had been happy with them.

Josquin had told her he had arranged for the rent on the apartment to be paid for six months in advance, without giving her any opportunity to protest. She wasn't sure what worried her the most: Josquin's high-handedness, or his assumption that she was staying that long or longer.

When she set Christophe down, he pulled himself to a standing position, clutching Sarah's hands to steady himself. His chubby legs made tentative walking movements. "Mam—mam—mam," he said in look-at-me tone.

She smiled at him. "You should be pleased with yourself, sweetheart. You'll be walking very soon."

She played with him until Perin returned for them. "The doctor says Prince Henry is well enough to see you, but you should avoid tiring him."

"I'll do my best."

Contrary to what Josquin thought, Sarah had come to realize she bore the old prince no malice. He was only doing what he thought was best for the province. In his place, Sarah knew she would do no less. The past two weeks had shown how quickly Valmont loveliness and peace became important to every person in the country.

Prince Henry looked worse than when she'd seen him a few days before. His head seemed sunken on his shoulders and his face was pasty. He clutched the oxygen mask in one hand, and used it to gesture to Perin and a nurse hovering near his chair. "Leave us."

When they were alone, he held out his arms. "Let me see my heir."

She placed the baby in the old man's arms, her reflexes set to catch Christophe if Prince Henry weakened. She needn't have worried. The old man's arms came around the child as if he'd been doing it all his life. He had been a father, she reminded herself.

"So you are Christophe," Henry said, chucking the baby under the chin.

The baby gave him a broad smile. Did he know that Prince Henry was his great-grandfather? In that moment, her nervousness at being in the ruler's presence fell away, replaced by a sense of family that made her feel choked.

Her heart ached for what they could have been to one another. "He looks like you," she said softly.

The old man was pleased, she saw, startled by the softening in his gaze. "Do you think so?"

She nodded, almost too emotional to speak. "He has your eyes."

"He does, doesn't he?"

Prince Henry sounded like every grandfather who ever lived, she thought. Where was the autocratic ruler now? "Christophe, this is your great-grandfather," she told the baby.

Christophe nodded as if he understood. "Pop-pop," he burbled.

She gave Prince Henry a helpless look. "He doesn't have many words yet."

"Pop-pop sounds fine to me. I'm pleased to be your pop-pop, Christophe."

If only Josquin could see this, she thought, then wondered if Prince Henry would have let his guard down so completely if they hadn't been alone.

Christophe began to play with the tubing leading to the mask, until Sarah gently untangled it from his fingers. "He must be getting heavy. Shall I take him?

"I'm not so far gone that I can't hold a baby," Prince Henry growled. "This child is the future of Valmont."

She tensed. "So Josquin informed me."

"Did he tell you my plans for Christophe?"

"I know he's the heir Valmont needs to retain its autonomy," she said.

The prince glared at her. "That goes without saying. I mean his future education."

She could hardly tell the old prince that she didn't plan to be in Carramer long enough for Christophe to begin his education, so she shook her head. "Josquin probably wants me to hear it from you." Especially if the news wasn't something she would like, she thought.

The prince snorted. "He's probably too busy romancing you, to keep his mind on affairs of state."

Remembering the effect of Josquin's kiss, Sarah felt color flood her cheeks. "With respect, I hardly think that's your concern, Your Highness."

"Everything in Valmont is my concern. Does he fancy you?"

She looked away, her face heating. Prince Henry read the truth she couldn't conceal. "In other words he does, but you still think I should have given your father my blessing to marry your mother."

Anger surged through her until she replayed his words in her mind. Should have? "What are you trying to say, Grandfather?" she asked, emphasizing the relationship.

"That I was a stubborn fool, and it cost me my son and his family. Are you satisfied now?"

She suspected it was as close to an apology from the old prince as she was likely to get. She wanted to rage that she deserved more, until she saw the gleam of wetness in his eyes. Raging wouldn't change the past. She took his hand. His skin felt papery and a tracery of veins showed through it. "I'm happy to know you, finally. And for Christophe to know where he comes from," she said, letting the anger go.

The old prince's fingers curled around hers, then released her. "You'd better take your son."

She lifted Christophe into her arms and rocked him as she sat down on the love seat opposite Prince Henry. The baby tugged at the pearl button of her blouse. She gave him the small stuffed horse she'd brought with her, and he fed the woolen strands of tail into his mouth. "You said you have plans for Christophe."

"I've appointed a royal nanny to take over his care immediately. When he is of age, tutors will supervise his education within the walls of the château."

When did Prince Henry plan to consult her? "I'm sorry but I can't agree, Grandfather," she said firmly, fearing that the moment of softness was over. "I'm the best person to care for him now, Later, he'll need the company of other children in a normal school environment."

"A prince's needs are different."

She thought of Josquin, and shook her head. "Christophe is my child first, and a prince second."

Prince Henry's arms gripped his chair. "There's nothing more to discuss. My decision is made. In time, you'll see that it's for the best."

"Whose best? Certainly not a tiny baby's. I won't have him cocooned in a palace, cut off from other children."

Henry straightened, looking ferocious. "That tiny

baby is my heir, and I'll decide what's best for him. And for you, for that matter.''

''We'll see, Your Highness.'' Was this what her real father had gone through, trying to convince Prince Henry that he loved her mother? Her heart bled for them.

The old prince jabbed at a button set into the arm of his chair. Moments later, the nurse reappeared.

Sarah began to fume. She couldn't argue with someone in Henry's condition. Yet how could she surrender her son to his dictates? She stood up, her arms tightening around the baby. Henry's body language made it clear the audience was at an end. She had little choice but to leave him alone.

When she returned to her suite, Josquin was waiting. He'd thrown his suit jacket over a chair back, and his tie hung askew. He looked tired, but still good enough to eat. ''How did the meeting go?'' he asked.

She settled Christophe into the playpen and arranged his horse and the alphabet blocks within reach. Over her shoulder she shot Josquin a savage look. ''How do you think it went? Did you know Prince Henry has appointed a nanny to take over from me?''

''All royal children have nannies.''

She straightened and almost collided with Josquin. Every nerve registered his nearness. ''Not this one.''

''You don't object when Maria or Perin assist with his care.''

''They're different. I think Henry means to separate me from my child altogether. You should have seen him. I'm sure he looks to Christophe to replace the family he lost.''

''You are the family he lost,'' Josquin pointed out. ''Henry has never forgiven himself for what happened to his son.''

She felt her lips tighten. "I know, he told me, more or less."

"If he admitted it, you've had more of an impact on him than you realize."

"Is that supposed to please me?"

"Can't you cut him a little slack, Sarina? He was brought up in a different world with different rules."

She tried to dodge past him, found him entirely too bulky and edged back until the playpen got in the way. "Don't call me Sarina."

"Sarah then." Josquin's hands itched to reach for her, so he hooked his thumbs into his belt. "Answer the question."

"I'll never accept Henry's plans for Christophe. My baby will not become a hostage to his ambition." Or yours, she was tempted to add.

"Are you sure that's what Henry wants?"

She planted her hands on her hips. "He as good as told me so. I might expect you to defend him. He thinks of you as a son. He even asked if you fancy me."

Josquin's eyebrow lifted. "What did you tell him?"

"I declined to answer. It's none of his business."

His finger traced a line along her jaw. "But it is *my* business."

She shuddered. Moving away seemed advisable, but she couldn't make her legs track. So she stayed put, swaying slightly as the light touch of his hand robbed her of breath.

"You know I fancy you," he said in a low voice.

She tried to shake her head, but only succeeded in nestling against his palm. His skin was smooth, warm. Her head felt too heavy to lift. "You hardly know me."

His lips skimmed her brow, and heat poured through her. "I've known you since Christophe was born."

A moan escaped her throat. She hoped he would mistake it for a protest. "I forgot about the photos. In America, we arrest people who spy on other people." His mouth had reached her jaw, and she shut her eyes, her senses swimming.

"So have me arrested," he said in a husky voice. "It's the only way you'll change how I feel when we're together."

He reached her mouth at last and claimed it hard. No teasing, no gentleness, only primitive male need, as dangerous as it was seductive.

Telling herself she shouldn't, she couldn't help but respond out of her own yearning to love and be loved. By him? She hoped not, but as his body pressed against hers, pleasure spiraled through her. Damn him, she did want him—fancy him, in Josquin's words.

She needed Josquin. Period. Holding her, kissing her, driving her to the brink of reason. She needed the touch of skin against skin, the fresh taste of his breath in her mouth, the pressure of his hands pulling her against him, leaving her in no doubt that the wanting was mutual.

He stroked her, held her, inflamed her. She held tight to him, skimming her hands along his shoulders and down his broad back, feeling muscles ripple beneath the fine lawn of his shirt. When his tongue probed her mouth, she gasped, feeling as if she stood on a precipice, saved from plunging to the depths only by his hold on her.

"No," she managed to say, struggling to place her palms against his chest. The sense of falling was terrifyingly real.

He held her for a moment longer, then stepped away, his face set. "We both know I'll accept no for now, but not for much longer."

"I won't be possessed by you."

"This isn't about possession. It's about a feeling stronger than either of us."

She gave a shaky laugh. "Ultimately between a man and a woman, it's always about possession. Only in my case, there's a province thrown in as well."

"How I feel about you has nothing to do with the future of Valmont."

"Doesn't it? Having me fall in love with you would be extremely convenient."

"I've already told you I don't want marriage."

"Yet you want me." Strange how much the words hurt to say.

His level gaze met hers. "Yes, I want you. More than I've ever wanted any woman."

"Because of my background, I'm not good enough for a prince, is that the problem?"

His hands curled around her upper arms, hot and biting. "Don't ever think so. My reasons for avoiding involvement have nothing to do with your background."

Fresh excitement tore through her, outweighing common sense. Move, she ordered herself, but stayed where she was. "I won't get involved with you," she denied on a shaky breath.

"I wouldn't ask you to. Kissing you was a mistake."

She feared they were about to make another one, but still couldn't make herself move away. "You haven't told me why."

He drew a deep, jarring breath. "I told you my mother was careless in her spending, but not the full extent of it. After my father died seven years ago, I discovered there was almost nothing left."

"I walked away from my inheritance. That should make us about even."

He gave her a wry look. "Our situations are hardly comparable. My mother looks to me to keep her in a style befitting a princess. The house she lives in must be maintained, and there are other estates with heavy mortgages that I can't sell because they're part of the national estate, and their staff depend on me." He raked a hand through his dark hair, his gaze deeply troubled.

She skimmed a hand along the side of his face, but withdrew as if burned. "I didn't know."

"No one else does, except a handful of close friends." He gave a sharp, mirthless laugh. "And our banker."

So he considered her close enough to take into his confidence? Her spirits leaped until she quelled them forcibly. "This isn't only about money, is it?"

"What do you mean?"

"People get married on a shoestring all the time. Are you sure pride isn't keeping you from following your heart? You had to struggle so hard that you won't let yourself get involved with a woman unless you can give her everything."

His gaze became shadowed, making her think she was probably right. Her heart ached for him, and for herself because his stubborn pride had created such a chasm between them.

"Then it's just as well we agree neither of us wants to get involved, isn't it?" he said stiffly.

"Absolutely."

He sounded about as certain as she felt, she thought, telling herself they were doing the right thing, the only thing. The attraction vibrating between them felt tangible, enticing. One slight move and she would be in his arms, his mouth on a fresh search and destroy mission.

She would be the one destroyed. And Christophe with her.

She moved away stiffly, like a sleepwalker, stopping when she reached one of the delicate antique chairs. She sat down, feeling her legs weaken. "I'm glad we understand each other. Now what am I going to do about Henry's plans for Christophe?"

Josquin looked shaken, too. She saw him make an effort to focus on her question. "In my experience, Henry usually gets his own way."

"Not this time. Growing up in a gilded cage may have been acceptable for royal children in Henry's time, but not for Christophe."

Hearing his name, Christophe had pulled himself up by the playpen bars, and held his arms out to Josquin. The prince lifted the baby out and jiggled him up and down, earning a delighted laugh.

They looked so good together, Sarah thought with a pang. Almost like father and son. She suppressed the image and got to her feet. "Let me take him. Your clothes…"

"Will clean," Josquin finished for her. He sat down with the baby on his knee and dangled a gold key chain in front of Christophe. The baby chattered to himself as he reached for the sparkling toy. Josquin looked up at her. "I can try to intercede with Henry on Christophe's behalf. It may help to remind him that even Prince Lorne has accepted the benefit of having his children attend a normal school and mix with other children."

Considering Josquin's loyalty to Prince Henry, this was a generous offer. She didn't like to think of Josquin incurring the old prince's wrath on their account, but couldn't offer a better alternative.

She took in a slow breath, making herself remember that Christophe's future was at stake. If Prince Henry had his way, her baby would be a prisoner of his heritage, and the price would be his freedom to grow and develop as a normal child. She couldn't let that happen.

She wanted to believe that Josquin could help, but he had already shown how loyal he was to the old prince. Could she trust him to intercede for Christophe? Henry was accustomed to getting his own way, ruling with an iron hand even from his sick bed. She had overheard Marie telling Perin that Henry could go on as he was indefinitely.

She kept her expression carefully impassive. "I need you to change Prince Henry's mind." But she knew she couldn't afford to wait. She and Christophe had to get away soon. A sharp sensation around her heart caught her unawares. Getting away should please her, surely? Instead she felt troubled, as if she would be leaving some part of herself behind.

Chapter Eight

Sarah could hardly believe that another week had passed since Josquin offered to speak to Henry for her. He had been as good as his word, confronting the old prince the next day. But Henry wouldn't be swayed. However, Josquin had managed to get Henry to delay appointing a full-time nanny until Christophe had settled in to royal life.

"We should be grateful for small mercies, shouldn't we, Chris?" she said to him as he splashed in his bath. His silken skin was sun-kissed and he looked a picture of health. Her heart snagged as she thought of someone imprisoning her precious child in a royal cocoon. How was she supposed to handle that?

She couldn't.

"Uck," he said, splashing at a floating bath toy.

She handed him the toy. "That's right, duck. Clever boy." He slammed it down on the water so it made an almighty splash, laughing uproariously as the backwash caught her.

She was forced to laugh, too, as she swabbed her face with a handy towel. "Next time you tell me to duck, I'll know you mean it."

She finished bathing him and wrapped him in a towel to carry him to his room. He kicked happily in her arms, trying out two more words he'd added to his vocabulary recently. "No," she understood, and was amazed at how accurately—and frequently—he managed to use it. But what was "Osh"?

She found out when Josquin joined them in the bedroom. He had taken to appearing each evening when she prepared Christophe for bed. He seemed to enjoy the ritual, although Sarah suspected he was also keeping an eye on them for Prince Henry.

Tonight Josquin was late. She had dried and powdered Christophe and was buttoning him into his sleeping suit when the prince arrived. At the sight of him, Christophe kicked happily. "Osh, Osh."

She slanted Josquin a curious look, putting two and two together. "Are you Osh?"

The prince looked sheepish. "Christophe couldn't get his tongue around Josquin, so while you were with your language tutor, I tried teaching him to say Josh. Friends call me that."

It suited him, she thought. But they weren't friends. Enemies didn't kiss one another. So what were they? She couldn't come up with an answer to satisfy her.

"So now you're Osh. He's been saying it all day, and I couldn't work out what he meant."

"Now you know."

"Christophe enjoys his time with you while I'm studying," she said.

He shook his head. "Marie and Perin will tell you I have as much fun as Christophe does."

All the same, his work was demanding. When she'd gone for a walk before bedtime, she'd noticed the light still burning in his office. He looked tired now. Fine lines radiated around his eyes, and faint shadows ringed them. As far as she could tell, most of his social activities revolved around his royal role. And with Prince Henry ill, many extra duties fell to Josquin.

The urge to smooth the lines away with her fingers, and press her lips to the grooves edging his generous mouth was so strong that she swayed toward him before she pulled back. He might be Christophe's friend, but she still didn't know where she stood with him. Not even where she wanted to stand.

"I want to invite you out tomorrow night," he said unexpectedly.

She ordered her thoughts with an effort. "A royal engagement?"

"My oldest friends," he said. "Peter Dassel and his wife, Alyce, are having a family dinner for their son's third birthday and I'm his godfather. I thought you might like to come along. You haven't set foot outside the royal compound since you came to Carramer."

Not a romantic occasion, she thought, feeling her spirits sag. What had she expected? "This compound is more like a city than a residence," she countered. "I've walked miles along the private beach, and seen the different royal homes, however a change would be nice. Other than Marie's baby, Christophe hasn't spent any time with other children since we got here."

"That's what I was thinking. Peter and Alyce also have one-year-old Gigi for him to play with."

"He'd enjoy that. I'm sure he misses the playgroup we used to go to."

"Then I'll collect you at five."

She was surprised to find how much she looked forward to the outing.

"Does Prince Henry mind us taking Christophe away from the château?" Sarah asked as they drove out through the wide wrought-iron gates. A uniformed chauffeur who also acted as a bodyguard was at the wheel, with a tinted partition separating him from herself and Josquin. Christophe sat happily in his special seat, his eyes huge as he followed the scenery through the window.

Josquin gave an irritable frown. "Carramer is a free country. Henry doesn't have to approve every move we make."

"Unless your son is his heir."

She was aware of Josquin's gaze settling on her. "I know this has been difficult for you."

More than he knew. "The language lessons are enjoyable, and the château is luxurious."

"That isn't what I meant."

She flashed him a look of anger. "Am I supposed to enjoy being watched whenever Chris and I set foot outside, knowing we'd be stopped if we tried to leave?"

"Carramer has its share of dissidents like any country."

She felt her mouth tighten. "Security is one thing. Being kept captive is quite another."

He turned to her. "The freedom of the country can be yours as soon as you give me your word that you won't try to take Christophe away."

"You would trust my word?"

"I believe you are a woman of honor."

"I like to think so." She fell silent, knowing he was right. She couldn't promise not to try to leave, when she intended to do so at the first opportunity. If he suspected as much, he didn't press the issue.

The Dassels lived about a half-hour drive from the château, along a spectacular coastal road lined with coconut palms. The sprawling, single-storied house with distinctive blue roof and shuttered windows overlooked a white sand beach, with the reef clearly visible and the lullaby of waves audible in the distance.

From her reading, she recognized that the house itself was classic turn-of-the-century Carramer in design, elegant and understated, with high, plantation ceilings, cherry wood furnishings, and cool, tiled floors. After the restrictions of Château de Valmont, she felt herself start to breathe again.

Josquin looked as if he felt the same, she noticed. He was casually dressed in charcoal pants and a shirt the color of wild honey, open at the neck. As soon as he was in the company of his friends, Peter and Alyce, Sarah saw the signs of stress drop away from his face as well. He looked vibrant, *happy,* she thought with a twinge of envy. The pull of attraction had never felt stronger.

After a wonderful, relaxed dinner, with the inevitable birthday cake and three candles for Marc, Josquin and Peter disappeared into a study. Talking business, Sarah assumed. When she said so, Alyce laughed. "The kind of business you conduct with snorkel and fins. They've been diving pals since their teens."

Another tidbit of information about him to file away. "Josquin didn't mention he liked diving."

"He didn't mention how lovely you are, either."

Sarah felt a blush start. "He probably hasn't noticed. Too busy making sure I learn how to be royal."

Alyce looked skeptical. Over dinner she and Peter had

learned how Sarah came to Valmont. "You had no idea at all that you were a princess, or that Christophe was the Valmont heir?" she asked now, her lovely lavender eyes wide.

Sarah shook her head. "I still feel as if I'm dreaming. How can a one-year-old baby be the heir to anything?"

Alyce looked at the children. Her daughter, Gigi, was babbling to Christophe in baby language, while the birthday boy was playing with a construction set Josquin had brought as his gift. Tonight's occasion was for grownups, Alyce had explained. A children's party for Marc's little friends had been held at his kindergarten earlier in the day.

"Christophe is a bit small for such responsibility," Alyce observed. "Growing up in Carramer, he'll have plenty of time to grow into his role."

Sarah had no intention of letting Christophe grow up here, but she kept the thought to herself. Alyce was trying to make Sarah feel at home. She didn't want to cause problems for the other woman, who was obviously fiercely loyal to Josquin. Deciding to change the subject, she asked, "How long have you known Josquin?"

Alyce brightened. "Josh and Peter were friends at college. I was on the college newspaper and asked Peter for an interview about his royal friendship. I was amazed when Josh volunteered to participate. I used to think being royal made you stuffy and unapproachable. But not Josh. Or you, for that matter."

Sarah smiled self-deprecatingly. "I haven't been royal long enough to know how I'm supposed to behave."

"Do you miss America?"

She hadn't missed her cramped apartment, or the daily struggle to provide for herself and Christophe. Occasionally she yearned for the simplicity of her life before she'd known she was adopted. "I miss the freedom to come and go as I please."

"There's a price for everything," Alyce said. She jumped up. "I'd better check on the coffee. Will you keep an eye on the children?"

"I'd love to." Being treated like a normal person felt good. She knelt on the floor beside Christophe. He also seemed to revel in the cosy domesticity, although she recognized that she was probably projecting her feelings onto him.

"Enjoying yourself?"

She looked up to find Josquin looming over her. "Peter had to take a business call. He's likely to be a while," he explained when she glanced around.

"Alyce is making coffee, so I'm baby-sitting."

Josquin dropped to the floor beside them, duly admiring the zoo that Marc announced he was building. "I could get used to this," he said.

"I was used to it. Perhaps not in such a glorious setting." Her gesture encompassed the ocean view from the floor-to-ceiling windows. The sunset had been spectacular, and now the sky was scattered with a thousand stars that looked close enough to touch.

"This was my life," she added.

He heard the reproach in her tone. "Until I wrenched you away from it."

She felt vibrantly aware of him sprawled within touching distance, looking completely at home surrounded by babies. The sort of man she could make a life with, had things been different.

They weren't different, as he'd just reminded her. "Being given no choice is what bothers me the most."

He propped himself on one elbow. "And if you *had* been given a choice?"

"I'd still want to know who I am and where I come from, without necessarily taking the knowledge any further."

He touched a hand to her hair. "Would the bare facts be enough for you? Wouldn't you want the actual experience?"

The slight touch sent a shiver ghosting down her spine. Suddenly they were talking about more than her family history. "Some experiences can be addictive."

His gaze rested on her mouth, setting her pulse drumming. "Not all addictions are dangerous. Some are downright pleasurable, Sarina."

That name again, said on a sigh almost of longing. How could a name sound like an invitation? From him, it did. Was that why she resisted hearing it?

She played with Christophe's toes, earning a grizzle of disapproval. He was busy exploring the ribbons on Gigi's dress and clearly resented his mother interrupting. She pulled her hand back but in the process, brushed Josquin's thigh.

Her jerky reaction was more extreme than the slight contact deserved, but she couldn't help it. Breathing hard, she scrambled to her feet. "The children..."

Josquin uncoiled from the floor, coming up within inches of her. "They're happily engrossed in each other."

That left her and Josquin. Wordlessly she surrendered to the inevitable and let him brush his lips across her mouth in a quick, tantalizing imitation of a kiss. Fleetingly she tasted filet mignon, the acid tang of red wine and Josquin. If not for the children playing at their feet, she would have tasted a great deal more, she knew.

The sound of a door opening broke the spell. She dragged in a deep breath as Josquin moved away from her. "Everything under control?" he asked Peter in a voice she noted was less than steady. The experience wasn't one-sided then.

Their host nodded. His eyes were full of questions, but he kept them to himself. Just as well. Sarah had no answers for herself, far less anyone else.

Alyce served coffee and a Carramer liqueur that tasted of honey and ginger. Sipping it, Sarah watched Josquin. He relaxed the way a leopard relaxes, she thought. Wary, long limbs at ease but muscles primed. The taste of his lips lingered on her mouth, flavoring the drink. Was he thinking of her, too?

He looked up and caught her watching him. As if in answer, he saluted her with his coffee cup. Were they telepathic now? She looked away, feeling her face burn.

Before they had coffee, Alyce had suggested putting Christophe to bed in Gigi's room. He didn't waken when he was transferred to the limousine for the return trip to the château. How simple life was for him, at least for now, Sarah thought, watching him in the car's dim light.

"I like your friends," she said, desperate to impose some normalcy between herself and Josquin. Beyond that challenging look, he had hardly said a word to her since that moment when he had wanted to kiss her.

"They're easy to be around," he said now.

"They treat everyone the same, without ceremony," she said. "Although Peter seems to be a workaholic." He'd disappeared to take or make business calls several times during the evening.

"He's not usually so driven," Josquin explained. "But Corbin Rees will only be in the province for a short time, while we tie up a deal to replace several planes from the royal fleet."

She could hardly believe her ears. "Did you say Corbin Rees?"

Josquin sat up a little straighter. "You know him?"

"My father…adoptive father…gave him his first job. Corbin worked his way up to a position on the board before he decided he preferred building planes to developing land. I can't believe he's coming to Valmont."

"Peter and I are meeting him tomorrow morning. Why don't you come along?"

The hint of a plan was forming in her mind. Corbin traveled in a private jet, combining showcase and transportation in one. He was in her family's debt for giving him his start. If she could only convince him to take her with him when he returned to America… "I'd like to, if I won't be in the way," she said, schooling herself not to sound over eager.

"It's time you started to go out. The press have already been speculating about you."

She'd read some of the stories in the English language newspapers. "I know."

Josquin shifted to look at her. "They're enchanted with the idea that you're a lost member of the royal family who was discovered living in America."

"Some of the reports speculate that I'm your mistress," she said. She had wished there was some way she could set the record straight. But Josquin had told her that the royal family didn't comment on stories about themselves in the tabloid press. "You think they'd be more considerate, knowing I have a one-year-old child."

His fine mouth twisted. "Some less savory journalists have found a role for him as my love child."

Her gaze moved to the baby, sleeping in his capsule. "We should have the right of reply." She could tolerate rumors about herself, but not about a helpless baby.

Josquin frowned, misunderstanding. "I understand why you'd object to anyone thinking I was Christophe's father. You have good reason to hate me, Sarina."

Whatever she felt for him wasn't hate, she knew, struggling to ignore the way her heart picked up speed at the memory of his kiss. "I can't fault you for doing your duty," she said.

He looked gratified and a little surprised. "To put an end to the rumors, Prince Henry plans to proclaim Christophe as his heir as soon as possible."

And Josquin himself as the Crown Regent, she thought. No wonder he thought she should be seen in public. He probably couldn't wait to make his role official. She had to get Christophe away soon. Once their identity became widely known, she would have no chance of spiriting him out of the country. Seeing Corbin and enlisting his help took on a new urgency. "What time is the meeting?" she asked.

"Tomorrow at eleven. Is Rees the business dynamo he's reputed to be?"

She didn't want to talk about Corbin Rees to Josquin, not only because she might betray herself by her interest, but because she was afraid that most men paled beside Josquin himself. The limousine was spacious, but he felt entirely too close, his long legs colliding with hers when she moved without thinking. Each time it happened, heat powered through her, and the urge to touch him again became more compulsive.

He hadn't spoken of the kiss, but he hadn't needed to. Every time her gaze glided over his mouth, she tasted him anew. She found she could barely conjure up Corbin Rees's features, for seeing the man in front of her.

"Corbin is loyal to his friends, but utterly career-driven," she explained. "He was too impatient to com-

plete his schooling but couldn't find anyone to give him
a chance until my adoptive father spotted his potential
and gave him his start. After that, Corbin didn't look
back.''

''Were you lovers?''

Josquin's cold tone washed over her like a rogue
wave. ''Corbin was never interested in me in that way.''
For a foolish moment, she'd thought Josquin might be
jealous, but as usual, royal concerns were uppermost in
his mind.

''You sounded so anxious to see Rees that the possibility crossed my mind. So he's only a family friend?''

''Nothing more.'' Except perhaps her ticket out of
Carramer, she thought. Somehow, the notion wasn't as
comforting as she expected.

Josquin settled back against the cloud-soft leather upholstery. ''Then it will be my pleasure to bring two old
friends back together.''

Chapter Nine

What did one wear to run away? Sarah wondered. Californian weather would be a lot cooler than Carramer if they got back to the States—*when,* she corrected herself. But she couldn't dress too obviously for travel, without making Josquin suspicious. She had no idea how she would arrange to remain aboard the plane. She would think of something, she had to.

After some deliberating, she donned a designer pant suit in navy linen over a plain white T-shirt, and slipped her feet into Dior pumps. Prince Henry had been generous with the clothes he'd had Josquin provide for her to choose from, and she had felt a bit like a child in a candy store, until she remembered that their sole motive was to make her over for the benefit of the royal family.

Christophe also had more clothes than he had owned in his young life. Today she had dressed him in a diminutive one-piece sailor suit and matching leather shoes. The handmade outfit would serve as a memento of this time in their lives, she thought.

She felt a stab of anxiety. Was she doing the right thing, taking him away from what Josquin called his birthright? In Carramer, Christophe was a prince, heir to a fabulous fortune that included this château. What could she give him to compare, when they were back in California?

Freedom, she told herself resolutely. If Prince Henry had his way, Christophe would be quarantined from other children, and tutored privately in a hothouse environment that would stifle his freedom to be himself.

Henry's rules hadn't stifled Josquin, she thought, feeling her throat tighten as she considered how much his own man he *was*. His education had been less restrictive than the one Henry planned for Christophe, but she suspected even if it hadn't, Josquin wouldn't be any different. Henry might hold the constitutional reins, but Josquin was not above challenging Henry's opinions or beliefs, or her own for that matter.

He challenged more than her beliefs about royalty. He rocked her opinion of herself, she recognized. He made her feel beautiful, desirable, sexy. Finding out that she had been adopted, unwanted by her real parents, as she'd thought, had plunged her into a lonely abyss from which she only now felt herself emerging. Amazing what a kiss could do, she assured herself, but knew that the kiss mattered less than the man doing the kissing.

As she gathered her hair into a knot at her nape, catching the thick strands with a mother-of-pearl clip, she struggled to subdue the strange fluttering inside her. She wouldn't allow herself to feel anything for him other than physically, but that was almost enough to make her change her mind about leaving.

If not for the almost daily battles she'd had with

Henry over her wishes for Christophe's upbringing, she wasn't sure she would have the will to leave at all.

She had agonized needlessly, she found, when Josquin came to fetch her. "The day is going to be hot and there is little shade at the airport. Christophe will be more comfortable remaining here with Marie and Perin," he said in a tone that brooked no opposition.

Helpless anger washed through her. Josquin couldn't know what she had planned. "An outing will be good for him," she insisted.

"We'll take him out when we return from the meeting. I have a few hours free after lunch."

Without arousing suspicion, she had little choice but to leave her precious child in the care of the ladies-in-waiting, and try to mask her misery as she joined Josquin for the limousine ride to the meeting aboard Corbin Rees's private jet.

As usual when Josquin was on official business, his equerry shadowed them in a second car. The only time he had been absent was last night, when they visited Josquin's friends, and he'd informed her that the chauffeur was a member of the Royal Protection Detail, well able to take care of them in any emergency.

Peter was waiting for them in the VIP lounge. "Rees's jet has landed and is taxiing to the terminal," he informed the prince. "We can go aboard shortly."

Her excitement was tempered at being without Christophe. Now she had two obstacles to overcome, persuading Corbin to let them accompany him to America, and getting Christophe away from the château. One step at a time, she told herself.

Corbin was grayer and heavier than she remembered, but he looked well, and he hugged her with enthusiasm, although he looked startled when Peter presented her as Princess Sarina de Valmont.

He contained his curiosity until they were alone in the main cabin of the luxurious jet. The captain had taken Josquin and Peter on a tour of the cockpit. She had declined, saying the technicalities were beyond her, but really to gain a few minutes alone with Corbin. "Your mother told me you'd found out you were adopted, but she never mentioned that you have royal blood," Corbin said.

"That's because they don't know. I only found out myself a few weeks ago," she explained. Corbin placed a glass of wine in front of her. She touched the glass to her lips but didn't drink, wanting to keep her head clear. "I'm surprised they admitted the truth to you after keeping it from me most of my life."

Corbin leaned closer. "Your mother misses you, Sarah. She told me she regrets not telling you the truth a lot sooner, but your father made her promise not to say anything. Can I tell her that you've found your real family? It will mean a lot to her to know that you're happy."

"I would say yes, if it were true."

The tension in her voice wasn't lost on him. "You're not happy? Forgive me, but I thought from the way he looks at you, that you and Prince Josquin…" He let the implication hang in the air.

"He was the one who lured me to Carramer. I'm a virtual prisoner at Château de Valmont."

Corbin laughed uneasily. "You're looking well on your confinement."

"Please, Corbin, this is serious. We need your help." His brows lifted. "We?"

She put the glass down before the wine spilled from her shaking fingers. "I have a one-year-old son."

"Who is also a member of the Carramer royal family," Corbin concluded. She was thankful he didn't voice any of the questions that must be in his mind. "Why won't they let you leave?"

She shot a glance over her shoulder, but the door to the cockpit remained closed. "I'm not the one Josquin wants. My son is heir to the present ruler of Valmont Province."

Corbin's smile died. "What can I do? Take a message to your folks?"

"Take me and Christophe with you when you return to America."

The executive went pale. "You're asking me to defy the ruling family of Carramer?"

She touched his arm. "I know it's asking a lot. At the very least you'll lose them as customers."

He gestured dismissively. "Heck, Sarah, I couldn't care less about the sale. I'm more worried about both of us winding up in jail. I can't just spirit you out of here. There are formalities."

She clenched her hands so tightly that her fingernails bit into her palms. "Tell me what I have to do."

He thought out loud. "Without your father's help when I was starting out in business, I wouldn't be where I am today, so you deserve any help I can provide. I could put you on the manifesto as a member of my team. If I asked them to, any of my people would volunteer to remain behind while you take their place. Damned if I know how to explain away a baby, but give me time, I'll think of something."

The sound of voices warned her that Josquin and Peter

were coming back. "What do you need from me?" she asked urgently.

"Sit tight at the château until I call you. For now, all I need are your passports."

She went cold. "Josquin took them when we arrived. They're still in his possession."

Corbin looked anguished. "You won't get back into the U.S. without them."

"When do you leave?"

"I fly to Solano tonight for talks with Prince Lorne's people and some local suppliers. At the end of the week, I touch down in Valmont for a couple of hours to refuel before flying straight back to the States."

Not much time, but all she was going to get. "We'll be here with the passports by then." Somehow she would find a way.

Joining them, Josquin looked from her to Corbin as if he could sense the tension in the air, but he said easily, "Have you two had a pleasant visit?"

Josquin had explained to Peter that she and Corbin were old friends. Now Peter turned immediately to business. "We're impressed with your work, Rees. The engineering standards are extraordinary."

Corbin looked relieved to be back in safe territory. "Our planes are engineered to the highest international standards. Each aircraft is individually configured to suit the client's specifications."

Sarah let the conversation flow around her, her thoughts whirling in directions that had nothing to do with planes and engineering. How was she going to retrieve her documents from Josquin's possession? His apartment was adjacent to the one he'd given to her and Christophe, but he also had servants hovering all the time.

A thought came to her. Corbin had quickly formed the impression that she and Josquin were involved. Could the servants have arrived at the same conclusion? If so, they wouldn't question Sarah's presence in Josquin's private rooms. His ever-present equerry was hovering in the background now. She decided to do all she could to convince him that she and Josquin were an item.

She moved to a seat closer to Josquin so she could rest a hand on his arm. "I know my opinion wasn't sought, but this plane is breathtaking," she said in a soft voice.

Josquin frowned into the champagne he hadn't touched. "I'm glad you think so, because you and Christophe will probably use it more than Henry."

"Then you'll recommend adding it to our fleet?"

Her use of the word "our" in reference to the royal family was deliberate, and also the first time she'd verbally included herself. Wishing for a video camera to capture Josquin's stunned expression, she glanced at the equerry. The man could barely conceal his smile.

Her plan was working. She was counting on the amount of time he'd spent with her being noticed and talked about already.

Josquin moved out from under her hand, and stood up. "Peter will finalize the details, but yes, I can recommend the plane based on the specifications I've already studied, and what I've seen today."

She got up too, positioning herself so that her hip grazed his. "This is so exciting, Josh. My own private plane."

Electricity shot through her. Through him, as well, if the sudden tightening around his eyes and mouth was any indication. She hadn't called him Josh before, and he hadn't invited her to. She wondered if the name sounded as right to him as it did to her. This was only an act, she reminded herself, fighting to keep her reactions under control.

"I've arranged for lunch to be served aboard," Corbin informed them. "A further demonstration of the plane's capability to act as a flying embassy when required. You will stay, I trust?"

Josquin nodded, and Peter also gestured his assent.

Sarah saw her opportunity. "I hope you'll forgive me if I return to the château, Josh? Christophe needs to be fed, and truth to tell, I'm rather tired."

Josquin looked concerned. "Would you like me to accompany you?"

Her fingers tightened on his arm, the firm flesh beneath her grasp sending waves of heat through her. "Please stay, I'll be fine."

The prince gestured toward his equerry. "Gerard will see you safely back to the château."

"Thank you." She turned to Corbin. "And thank you for your hospitality. It was good to see you again."

Corbin gave her a forced smile. "Nice seeing you again, too, Your Highness."

The title sounded odd voiced in an American accent. Not for much longer, she resolved. "It's still Sarah between us," she insisted. "I hope I'll see you again soon."

Corbin inclined his head in acknowledgment of what she was really saying. She *would* see him again soon. If she could possibly manage it, she and Christophe would be aboard his plane and on their way to America by the end of the week.

She was aware of Josquin's speculative gaze on her as she followed the equerry down the steps of the plane, but she steeled herself not to look back.

Chapter Ten

Sarah never thought she would be happy to return to the château, but this time she could hardly wait for Josquin's equerry to escort her to her suite, and be gone.

She took care of Christophe's needs, regretting that she couldn't afford to spend time playing with him, as she usually did when they'd been apart. She hoped he somehow understood that she was doing this for him.

"I'm planning a surprise for Josquin, so I have to leave Christophe with you for a little while longer," she told Perin with what she hoped was a secretive smile.

The lady-in-waiting gave her a curious look, but was too well trained to comment. "As you wish, Your Highness."

Rank had its privileges, Sarah found herself echoing Josquin's comment as she hurried along a wide corridor toward the wing the prince occupied when he resided at the château. She had asked him about his real home, but hadn't received a proper answer. Perhaps his home had been a casualty of his financial difficulties, so he didn't like discussing it. Compassion for him tugged at her, until she willed it away.

Josquin's apartment was as impersonal as a hotel suite, she found when she slipped inside. As she had anticipated, the equerry was there, rearranging books on a shelf. "Can I help you with something, Your Highness? Prince Josquin has not yet returned."

Sarah imitated Prince Henry's imperious attitude. "Thank you, Gerard. I shall take a bath and wait for him here." She let her gaze travel to the massive four-poster visible through an open set of carved doors. Slowly and deliberately, she shed her jacket and draped it over a chair back. Then she lifted her arms and released the clip from her hair, shaking the curls out around her shoulders.

Not by so much as a muscle did Gerard's expression change, but she saw alarm come into his eyes. As if he feared she was about to remove anything more, he said hastily, "As you wish, ma'am. I can finish this later." With a bow, he saw himself out.

His face was a study, she thought. If the situation hadn't been so serious, she would have laughed. The equerry was totally convinced she was more than a guest to Josquin. How long before word of this latest development spread among the rest of the staff?

She wouldn't be around to worry, she thought, dismissing her feeling of concern. She had no idea when Josquin might return, so the sooner she located the vital travel documents, the better.

The salon was a twin of her own, but decorated in more masculine style with dark furnishings, Persian carpets and ponderous oil paintings on the walls. She couldn't believe they were Josquin's choice. He would prefer scenes of nature at its most untamed, she thought, not sure how she knew. The ocean in storm, a deer in full flight. Such subjects seemed to suit his style better than ancestral portraits.

Concentrate on your task, she ordered herself, aware of the difficulty when Josquin seemed so close. A book lay open on a chair and she looked at the title. *The Brothers Karamazov.* So he read the classics. That his choice should be one she considered a great romance sent a shiver of recognition down her spine. The book was one of her favorites.

She tore herself away. A substantial bureau sat in an alcove, the roll top open. A notebook computer was open on top, incongruously modern among a sheaf of heavy parchments bearing the royal coat of arms. She left them alone, feeling guilty enough for snooping, without going through what were obviously state papers. A thorough check of the drawers revealed no sign of her own documents.

Where else could they be? She hesitated at the door of his bedroom, feeling like an invader in his personal space. The room was a model of neatness, the only personal touch a battered teddy bear sitting atop a side table. Her lips curved into a smile. The childhood relic made Josquin seem alarmingly human, and disturbingly close. She perched on the end of the bed, wondering where to start.

"Looking for something, Sarina?"

Her heart jumped in her chest. She looked up to find Josquin leaning indolently against the door post. His relaxed posture didn't fool her. There was fire in his eyes.

She kept her head high, although she trembled inwardly. Because he had caught her snooping, or because he had found her in his bedroom? She didn't stand, mainly because she didn't want to find out whether or not her legs could hold her. "I wanted to see what your apartment was like."

He moved toward her. "Gerard told me, discreetly of course, that you were waiting for me in my bedroom. Am I to assume that you've finally accepted your situation? Perhaps even started to enjoy it?"

He spoke softly, seductively, his voice making her think of hot chocolate, rich burgundy wine and sex. His hand grazed the side of her face, pushing her hair back with a gesture so intimate that she almost leaped out of her skin. She tried to get to her feet, instinctively needing to meet him on equal terms, but he forestalled her by placing his arm around her.

In one fluid movement he joined her on the bed, and swept her backward until she lay alongside him, held in the curve of his arm. She couldn't move and she could hardly breathe for the tension swirling inside her.

She tried to meet his gaze and failed. "Gerard misunderstood me."

Josquin stroked the side of her face, his fingers threading through her hair. "What part of 'waiting in my bedroom' didn't he understand?"

Under the hand she pressed against his chest, she felt his heartbeat quickening. Her own pounded no less erratically. She had wanted this, she recognized on some level. The need to see where Josquin slept had driven her as strongly as the wish to find her travel documents.

Why hadn't she been more honest with herself? The attraction had been instant and powerful, from the first time she saw him stride into the customs hall. Every second she had spent in his company since then had brought her a step closer to this moment. She didn't think she had wanted him to discover her in his bedroom, but could she trust her own motives? If she wasn't careful, she would imagine herself in love with him.

"I simply meant I wanted to talk to you, privately," she tried, hearing her voice shake.

He didn't move. His body felt hot and hard against hers. "Is this private enough?" he murmured, skimming her forehead with his lips.

Something snapped awake inside her. She *had* wanted this, courted it, dreamed of Josquin touching her like this, she recognized. Was her so-called scheme no more than simple wish fulfillment? She had never been in love. Lust, yes, but this felt different. More all-consuming, as if she could burst into flames at any moment. Was she falling in love with Josquin, against all common sense?

Josquin saw the shock come into her eyes. Their serene gray-green coloring became stormy and troubled. Because of him? He didn't like the thought one bit. He bent to kiss her, wanting to assuage her panic.

As his mouth closed over hers, he heard her sharp intake of breath, but her lips parted. The soft moan starting deep in her throat almost stopped him until he heard the invitation there. He deepened the kiss. She closed her eyes but he kept his open, savoring her extraordinary beauty. The château held treasures of world renown, but none to compare with the woman in his arms.

Her hair spilled over his arm in glorious waves. She had thrown her head back, exposing an expanse of creamy throat that made him mindless with longing. No wonder vampires were such a persistent myth even in Carramer. The urge to taste that delicate flesh with his teeth was almost overpowering.

He could hardly believe that a woman like Sarah existed in his world. Her skin glowed like the delicate porcelain used at court on the most special occasions. Her impossibly long lashes fluttered against her cheeks. If she opened her eyes, he would see stars in them, he was certain. He could feel the stars in his own.

He wanted her, yearned for her, touching her with an urgency that felt driven, as if touch alone could satisfy the desire raging through him. Caressing her was a voyage of discovery, satisfying him for now, although he knew not for long.

Under his questing fingers, her skin quivered as he awakened nerves, teased responses. When he traced the fullness of her lips, her mouth closed over his finger. Pleasure-pain speared to the very center of his being.

He had to kiss her again. She tasted wonderful, like the finest wine. Her perfume swirled around him, clouding his senses. Barely able to breathe, he massaged her breasts, the hardening points through the thin shirt firing him with desire.

He had dreamed of this since being captivated by the photos of her before she came to Carramer. His task hadn't required him to study every graceful movement, or learn her habits and her responses, until the very essence of her was burned into his memory. He had done it because he couldn't help himself. She had been his dream woman, and now she lay beneath him, returning his kisses as he had fantasized she would. He was a heartbeat away from making her his own.

He heard the readiness in her throaty cries, and felt her surrender in her mindless response to his touch. Impatiently he pushed the shirt up until he found the fastening of her bra. The flimsy garment clasped in front, offering little impediment to his restless exploration. The fullness of her breasts spilling into his hands threatened his sanity.

Her eyes opened but were glazed, as he touched his fill. Her back arched to meet him, sending his senses into a flurry of needs that felt like knives slicing through his body. He ached with wanting her.

She matched him need for need, turning sideways until she was crushed against his hardness, as if she couldn't get enough of him, either. Her mouth under his was hungry, seeking, her tongue tangling with his in a duel of seduction that gave no quarter. He asked none, offered none, and didn't think she wanted him to. There was only one way this could possibly end.

He stood and gathered her into his arms, lifting her, swirling her around the room as he plundered her mouth. He thought to end the dance at his bed where finally, finally, he would know her fully, exploring all that she promised and giving everything of himself to her in return.

He stopped at the bed, held to coherence by the merest thread. What in the name of thunder was he doing? What had happened to his lofty vow to give himself to no woman while he had so little to offer her?

Sarah's look was troubled, as she felt his mood shift. "What is it, Josquin? What's wrong?"

He placed her carefully on the bed, as if she could break, well aware that he was the one who might. "*This* is wrong." She had been placed in his care. The tremors pouring through him told him how close he had come to betraying that trust, to betraying himself and her. He felt his expression turn to ice as he looked at her, realizing that he had never come closer to losing control.

He took a step away from the bed, unable to trust himself if he remained so close. "Get up," he said, not sure if he was asking her or pleading with her.

She struggled to her feet, tidying her clothes with dig-

she was glad he didn't suspect her real motive felt oddly unconvincing. What was the matter with her? She should be glad he hadn't guessed the truth. Instead, she felt his rejection as keenly as a knife to the heart.

She drew herself up, determined not to let him see how badly he had hurt her. "You're right."

Something flickered in his expression. Satisfaction, probably, because he was right, or thought he was. She refused to recognize the flicker as disappointment. He could only be disappointed if he cared, and she had just seen, in the most humiliating way, that he didn't.

His face turned stony. "You know yourself that talking to Henry won't help. He insists that Christophe be raised in the traditional royal way."

Which she wouldn't allow. "There must be some way to change his mind."

"There is one possibility."

Unless she could locate their travel documents, she couldn't get Christophe away. She had to do something. "Tell me what it is."

"Marry me."

She stared at him blankly. "What?"

"Agree to become my wife. As Christophe's father, my wishes for your son's future would take precedence over Prince Henry's."

Her mind spun in a thousand different directions as she tried to come to terms with what Josquin was suggesting. Marry him? Could she contemplate such a step, even for her child's sake? The silence stretched between them as he waited for her answer.

Chapter Eleven

Josquin watched uncertainty, apprehension and then the shock of possibility chase each other across Sarah's delicate features. He wondered if she knew how transparent she was to him. Playing poker with her would be entertaining, but rather one-sided, he suspected.

His own emotions were hardly tranquil but royal life had given him a lot more practice at concealing them. He had surprised himself as much as Sarah by proposing marriage. He was the wrong man to offer her any such thing. But he couldn't make himself regret it. Nor was he convinced that his motive was purely to protect Christophe.

Josquin gave vent to a restless sigh. When had his life become so complicated? From the moment Sarah entered his life, came the undeniable answer. His first sight of her photograph had hit him like a thunderbolt. Actually meeting her had swept aside the last remnants of his ability to remain aloof.

She challenged him in a way no woman had ever

done, excited him, aroused him. These days, she haunted his dreams. The thought of another man possessing her made him crazy. He was deadly afraid that if she left, she would leave a void in his life that no one else could fill.

When had she become so important to him? He couldn't say, except that she had. He refused to accept that what he felt was love. There was no room in his life for such a luxury. But he needed her. That he might need her the way a man needs to go on breathing to live, he didn't want to consider.

She was wrong about him being ambitious to succeed Henry. Josquin had never entertained such an idea, and didn't like to do so now. Until he had located Christophe, Josquin had assumed that, as Carramer's present monarch, Prince Lorne would become ruler of Valmont under the terms of the ancient charter. Finding a male heir to the province had changed everything.

Henry's unpredictable state of health and the fact that his heir was an infant, meant Josquin had little choice but to prepare himself to become Crown Regent if the worst happened. He didn't expect Sarah to understand, having been raised outside the royal family. Josquin didn't have to like it, but his duty had to come first.

Sarah's father had accepted his duty. The cost had been Philippe's heart and ultimately his life, and this understandably horrified Sarah. Josquin might not approve, but he understood. Some things were beyond personal choice.

So what was he doing asking her to be his wife? Wasn't he putting his own desires ahead of his duty? He might delude himself that he was acting out of concern for Christophe, but Josquin knew his motives were far more personal.

For a heartbeat he hoped that Sarah would say no, then chided himself for expecting her to let him off the hook. If she agreed, he would have to keep his personal feelings out of the arrangement, however difficult the task. Looking at her, so utterly beautiful and desirable, he suspected it was right next door to impossible.

So be it. He'd tackled the impossible before, when he undertook the task of rebuilding the family fortune. He hadn't told Sarah, but one of his carefully planned investments looked like bearing fruit earlier than he had expected, and would go a long way to regaining his family estate. After the estate was unencumbered, he might be able to let his proposal of marriage mean something. Until then, a marriage of convenience was all he had any right to offer Sarah.

The thought of making her his wife in name only was so unexpectedly painful that this time, he did have to struggle to disguise his feelings, as he said, "Have I given you such a difficult choice?"

"You must know you have," Sarah defended herself, her mind and her senses whirling. For a giddy moment she saw herself as Josquin's wife. She had tasted enough of his kisses to believe that he would be a lover without equal. She had no doubt he would be a considerate husband in other ways, too. If only he had proposed to her out of love instead of ambition.

Temptation gnawed at her. Yes, her heart sang. No, her logical mind denied. She moved to the window and looked out, noting distantly that Josquin's suite had an ocean view that was the twin of hers. The restless waves mirrored her turbulent state of mind. "You can't expect me to answer such an astonishing proposal right away. I need time to think," she prevaricated.

He made an impatient sound that belied his next

words. "Take all the time you need. Only pray that Henry makes no irrevocable decisions about Christophe's future while you're making up your mind."

She flinched at the low blow, but knew he was right. She spun around to find him almost at her shoulder. Her heart hammered painfully, and she took an involuntary step backward. "I thought you don't want to marry while your fortunes are in disarray."

He frowned as she retreated from him, but moved away and braced himself against the antique desk. "I don't want to marry for love," he agreed. "Convenience is another matter. As a princess in your own right, you need have no expectations of me beyond ensuring we share the right to control your son's future."

What a cold bargain he was offering. She tried to tell herself she was pleased. Hadn't she also promised herself she wouldn't become romantically involved while Christophe depended on her? The deal should suit her admirably. So why did she feel as if the sun had gone in on her day? "What would you expect in return?" she asked.

He regarded her gravely. "Your faithfulness and your silence."

She lifted her head, letting him see in her eyes how hurt she was that he would think he needed to demand that she be faithful to him. He might not love her, but she would honor her marriage vows. Anything less was simply not in her character. His other request was more puzzling. "My silence? In what way?"

"As a de Marigny, I don't need Henry's permission to marry, and Prince Lorne is not likely to withhold his blessing. But if Henry suspects that our marriage is a conspiracy against his authority, he has the constitutional power to order the arrangement annulled. If we do marry, you must be prepared to act the part of my loving wife for as long as Henry lives, in the bedroom as well as out of it.''

''Why *in* the bedroom?'' she stammered. Picturing herself as Josquin's lover was one thing. Having him boldly declare he intended them to share a bedroom was quite another. ''Surely, we can do as we choose behind closed doors?''

''There are few secrets in royal circles,'' he pointed out. ''Were you and I to sleep apart, palace gossip would carry the news to Henry so fast your beautiful head would spin. He would soon put two and two together.''

She dragged in a difficult breath. The room seemed empty of oxygen suddenly, the bed visible through the open door looming large, especially in her mind. Could she really agree to share so much, knowing all the feeling was on her side? She struggled to think rationally. ''Throughout history, royal couples have slept apart. Queen Victoria and Prince Albert for example. There must be others.''

''They didn't have Prince Henry scrutinizing their every move.'' Josquin cut across her. ''As things stand, he's likely to do everything in his power to thwart our marriage plans.''

Belatedly she understood the enormity of what Josquin was prepared to risk to help her. ''You'd really incur his anger on our account?''

''I accept that Prince Henry's plans for Christophe are wrong. If I can do something to change them, I will.''

He was doing this for Christophe, not for her, she understood. By marrying her, Josquin would cement his position as the future regent. The thought didn't stop her heart from hammering against her ribs. He would still be her husband, and the intimacy the prospect entailed took her breath away.

She funneled her panic into concern for Josquin. "Henry means so much to you. Are you sure you want to cross him?"

Josquin's look was wry. "Henry has been my mentor since I was a teenager. I am more grateful to him than you can possibly imagine. But every child has to grow up sometime. Leaving home is not simply a physical act. The separation must be mental as well. Taking your side against Henry is part of that."

All the same, she was awed that Josquin meant to stand up for her and Christophe against the one person who meant most to him in the world. "No one has been willing to make such a sacrifice for me before," she said, struggling to rein in the tremor in her voice.

He heard it and came closer, taking her gently into his arms. At his touch, a shudder rippled through her, and she recognized it as pure, wanton desire.

"Have you looked in a mirror lately, Sarina? My proposal is not so self-sacrificing as you might think. Since I won't marry for the usual reasons, you are a gift to me as well. You will make a fitting bride for a prince."

He turned her until she was facing a gold-framed cheval mirror opposite the window. The image was like a portrait seen on the cover of an impossibly romantic novel. Against the vividly painted ocean backdrop, Josquin stood behind her, his hands resting lightly on her shoulders. In the golden light, his features looked carved from stone, but his eyes held a flame she hadn't seen before.

She barely recognized herself in the reflection. She'd never thought herself beautiful, but she looked radiant. Could being in Josquin's arms make such a difference to her appearance? How else could she explain the way her skin glowed and her mouth settled into the softly mysterious smile of a woman who knew she was desired?

Desired but not loved, she reminded herself forcibly. He wasn't offering her love. Not even physically. He had only insisted they share a marital bed for appearances' sake. Could she live with such a bleak bargain?

For Christophe's sake, she had no choice. She couldn't let Henry take over her child's upbringing. If she couldn't find a way to get them away from Carramer, Josquin's proposal offered the only possible solution. She took a deep, steadying breath and turned away from the mirror, away from the revealing radiance in her expression. Time to face reality. "Yes, I will marry you," she said in a voice she was proud to hear shook only a little.

He heard it anyway. "There's no need to fear our bargain. I may not be a good provider in the material sense, but I intend that to change. In the meantime, I will be your bulwark against Henry and the whole world if need be."

She shook her head. "Christophe and I have survived on very little for the last year. We can do it again if we must. Your advocacy means much more to me."

His eyes sparkled. "You see me as a knight in shining armor, Sarina?"

She didn't like to think how well he fitted the role. "When will you tell Henry?"

"Soon. First we need to lay some groundwork to allay any suspicion."

She gave him an uncertain look. "What kind of groundwork?"

"To convince Prince Henry that we're madly in love."

"Oh." She should have expected something of the sort, but she was taken by surprise when he pressed his lips to hers. Her blood heated instantly, filling her veins with liquid fire. She was trying to absorb the impact when he stepped away from her. Covering her discomfiture with a nervous smile, she said, "What was that for? There are no witnesses here."

He measured her with a look. "Can you be certain?"

As if on cue, Josquin's equerry, Gerard materialized behind them. Sarah started. She hadn't heard the man come in. Josquin must have done, and had kissed her to signal their new relationship. He had wanted his equerry to see, and probably report back to the other staff. A knot of anger twisted inside her. She didn't like the thought of Josquin kissing her for show.

What did she expect, genuine passion? she asked herself, as angry with herself as with him. He was only standing by their agreement. And she didn't like the equerry sneaking up on her. "Don't do that," she muttered, unable to help herself.

The man frowned his confusion. "Your Highness?"

Josquin stepped between them. "Everything's fine, Gerard. The princess and I are just on our way out."

"We are? I mean, we are."

Josquin indicated his business suit. "If we're going swimming, I'll need to change, darling."

She finally got the message. "I'll change and get Christophe ready, too."

When she rejoined Josquin twenty minutes later, he looked relaxed and impossibly handsome in an open-necked shirt in a navy and white Carramer design somewhere between Batik and Hawaiian. White shorts made his legs look longer and more muscular than usual. Leather sandals had replaced his business shoes. Her stomach knotted at the thought of becoming wife to this prepossessing man.

She had changed into a white linen sundress with shoestring straps, over a white one-piece swimming costume. She had knotted her hair on top of her head, and carried a raffia sun hat. She had also dressed Christophe for the sun. He bounced impatiently in his stroller.

"Aren't we going to the beach?" she asked, when Josquin started to lead the way along a coral path to the swimming pool.

"Henry takes the air on his balcony at this time most afternoons. His apartment overlooks the pool," he explained.

So the outing was purely for the old prince's benefit. She knew they needed to convince Henry that theirs was a genuine love match, but she felt disappointed. Wanting Josquin to really want to spend time with her? Fool, she chided herself. Better get that fantasy out of her head right now.

She was a princess. Royalty made marriages for reasons other than love. Get used to it. Never, a voice in her mind denied. She silenced it with a frown. Josquin saw and frowned back. "Something wrong?"

Everything.

"Nothing," she said, and fussed with Christophe in the stroller.

"I have to stop by my office and pick up my sunglasses, it won't take a moment."

"We'll come with you." She wanted to see where he worked, what he did when the light she had seen from the garden burned late into the night.

His office was light and airy, with French doors opening onto the gardens. In the outer room, a bevy of staff worked industriously, hardly looking up when Josquin strolled in, although she saw them shooting interested glances at her and Christophe. She kept her back straight and followed Josquin into his sanctum.

There was more of him here than in the apartment at the château, she saw. The furniture was less ponderous, more modern. The latest electronic equipment littered the desk, looking well used. Files carried names like Business Council and the logos of internationally known companies. She saw a file for Corbin Rees's planes on top of one stack.

She moved to a glass-fronted cabinet, admiring a collection of trophies engraved with Josquin's name and various athletic achievements. Christophe wobbled on his chubby legs at her side, his hand clutched in hers. She smiled as he stood nose to nose with his reflection in the glass. "Me."

"Yes, that's Christophe, sweetheart," she assured him. She read the plaque on the nearest trophy, and looked over her shoulder at Josquin. "Shooting?"

Josquin grinned ruefully. "Shooting was considered a necessary royal accomplishment. I haven't done any for fifteen years, and then only at targets."

She let her relief show. "You don't hunt foxes or anything?"

"Wrong royal family. There are no foxes in Carramer."

"I'm glad." She turned his attention to his desk and something froze inside her as she spotted a familiar-looking bundle of documents. Her travel papers. Her heart thundering, she lifted Christophe onto the edge of the desk. He reached for a leather-bound folder. She leaned across and pushed the folder out of his reach. "No, sweetheart, mustn't touch."

"Don't worry, he can't do much damage." Josquin turned his back and moved toward a bookshelf. His sunglasses were perched on top.

Without giving herself time to think, she snatched up the travel documents and slid them into her beach bag. Then she gathered Christophe into her arms, burying her face in his tummy to hide her flaming features.

Josquin turned around. "Ready?"

She managed to nod as she gathered the baby into her arms. Yes, she was definitely ready now.

Chapter Twelve

Somehow she got through the next hour at the pool, although she had trouble convincing herself that Josquin didn't know that the documents were in her bag. Acting normally was as hard as anything she had ever done.

"You're really nervous about this," he said when they emerged from the water.

She fumbled with the fastenings of the floating baby seat Josquin had provided for Christophe to enjoy the water. She had never seen anything like the useful device. Christophe had liked it so much that she made a mental note of the brand name, Jaydem, in case she was able to purchase one for Christophe when she returned home.

Now the harness resisted her shaking fingers. "What do you mean?"

Josquin moved her aside and undid the device without difficulty. He lifted Christophe out and cradled him against his chest. They looked perfect together. Both lean and long-limbed, both disturbingly handsome, and so at home with one another that her insides clenched in protest.

Christophe found Josquin's dark hair fascinating, and tangled his fingers in the wet locks. Josquin didn't seem to mind.

"I mean making Henry think we're in love," Josquin said.

Relief coursed through her. He didn't know about the documents at all, and had arrived at his own explanation for her nervousness.

She looked away so he wouldn't read the truth in her expression. "The idea does take some adjusting to."

When they arrived the old prince had been seated on a balcony overlooking the pool. Josquin had made a great show of settling Christophe into the flotation device, putting an arm around Sarah to demonstrate how the device worked. He had even kissed her lightly before helping her into the pool and handing Christophe down to her. She'd been glad the baby seat supported Christophe in the water, when it was all she could do to absorb the impact of a simple kiss.

When Josquin joined her in the pool, he had acted exactly as she imagined a loving fiancé would behave, touching her at every opportunity, and once, coming up beneath her and lifting her into his arms to kiss her again.

His body had been slick and warm, his hold irresistible. Her arms had linked around his neck almost of their own accord. Awareness had shivered through her, hot, strong and undeniable. If not for Christophe splashing happily nearby in his safety seat, and the knowledge that they were under Prince Henry's eye, she didn't know what would have happened next.

She wasn't sure what effect Josquin's behavior was

having on Prince Henry, but she doubted if she would ever breathe normally again. When Josquin released her with what she could swear was reluctance, but could only be more play acting, the water caressed her skin in imitation of his touch, triggering the wish that he would touch her more often, kiss her more deeply.

Love her?

She shook the idea off as she had shaken the water off herself when she emerged from the pool. Love wasn't part of their agreement. He wasn't offering it, and she didn't require it, did she?

She didn't need anyone to take care of her. Since leaving her adoptive parents' home two years ago, she'd managed just fine. Josquin had caused the problem with Prince Henry by luring her to Carramer under false pretenses. Proposing marriage was the least he could do to help her out.

She couldn't help it if his kisses put ideas in her head that had no business being there. He was a prince, for pity's sake, a fairy-tale figure who was bound to turn any woman's head.

He'd done everything just right, from making friends with her child, to interceding for them with Prince Henry. Was it any wonder that he managed to haunt her thoughts, day and night?

She was *not* lonely, she assured herself. She had her friends at the art gallery where she used to work, the mothers of the children at the playgroup where she took Christophe once a week. And...

And that was it, she acknowledged on an inward sigh. As a McInnes, she'd been a social asset, invited to everything, courted by the sons of her family's friends. As a single mother with no particular social standing, she'd spent more evenings at home watching television than whirling around a dance floor.

Living in the luxurious surroundings of the château, being treated as a princess, was more exciting than anything she'd done in over a year. She was bound to be more vulnerable than usual to Josquin's charm. That had to be why she was finding him so hard to get out of her mind.

The sooner she and Christophe returned to their normal lives, the sooner she could relegate Josquin to his proper place in her memory. A wonderful memory, granted. But with no more relevance to her real life than any holiday romance.

Yeah, right, she thought. She might manage to forget Valmont, but forgetting Josquin was going to be much more difficult. Especially if he insisted on smiling at her the way he was doing now. In spite of her best intentions, she felt her insides begin to melt.

"Do you think you could unravel this child from my hair while I still have some left?" he asked good-humoredly.

She wished there was some way she could comply from a distance, without having to step closer and inhale the steamy male fragrance he exuded that made her think of long nights and tangled sheets.

What was she doing? He had proposed to her for a reason, a good, sound, practical reason. She had accepted for the same sound, practical reason. Letting herself imagine intimacies that had nothing to do with their agreement was a recipe for disaster.

She stepped up to him, ignoring the sudden fast pounding of her heart. "No, Christophe, let go." She began to release the black strands from around her child's fingers.

"Ow," Josquin protested. "At least the baby was gentle."

"Would you like me to leave him as he is? Two babies are more than I can handle." Josquin would always be more than she could handle, she sensed.

He gave a rueful grin. "Point taken. Go ahead and do your worst. I can stand it."

She was more careful this time as she unwound Josquin's hair from Christophe's fingers. As she lifted the baby away, he howled a protest. "No! Osh," and stretched out toward the prince.

She jiggled the baby against her hip, wondering how Josquin had managed to capture her son's heart so quickly. Her own awareness of him bordered on obsession. "Hush, sweetheart. You can play with Josh's hair another time," she murmured.

The prince set his ruffled hair to rights with his fingers. "Don't I get some say in this?"

"Not if Christophe wants you for a plaything."

"And what about his mother? Does she want me for a plaything, too?"

She glanced up at the balcony, and back to Josquin, her pulse racing. "Don't be ridiculous. Prince Henry isn't watching us now."

Josquin's dark gaze settled on her. "You think I only asked because of Henry?"

"Our agreement…"

"Doesn't stop us from enjoying ourselves," he pointed out with maddening logic. "Do you think your son could spare you for tonight, if I took you out dancing?"

Odd that she had been thinking about dancing only minutes before. "In the interests of making our engagement look real?"

"Definitely," he agreed, sounding as if he found the idea amusing.

His invitation was so appealing, so exactly what she needed, that she decided against any more analysis. "I'd like to go dancing," she said solemnly.

"I'll collect you at eight. That should give you time to see Christophe settled for the night, and do whatever you need to do before going out on the town."

"What makes you think I want to do anything special for you?" she asked, aware that she was falling into a teasing mood with him that was not only unwise, but downright reckless.

His assessing look roved over her, heating her blood. "You can go exactly as you are now, and I won't mind." He brushed a damp strand of hair off her face, his fingers lingering on her cheek as if reluctant to break the contact.

The touch was so slight yet so intimate that her throat seized. If she hadn't seen Prince Henry go inside, she could have believed Josquin's gesture was purely for show. Harder to explain when he had no reason to touch her. Harder still to explain her traitorous response.

"I'll be ready," she managed to whisper, wondering what exactly she would be ready for.

He came precisely at eight. Most men looked good in a dinner jacket. Josquin looked breathtaking. His was midnight blue with gleaming satin lapels, over a dress shirt white enough to dazzle. But the man inside was what held her wondering gaze.

The suit was obviously of the finest quality, but no amount of expert tailoring could create such beauty, if that was the right word for a man. For he *was* beautiful. Also strong, handsome, intelligent and dangerous. Her pulse quickened at the same time as a tug of desire gripped her. Beautiful *and* dangerous. A combination to be handled with care.

Or not handled at all, if she had any sense.

He saw her looking around as they waited for his car to be brought to the entrance. "Missing something?"

"Shadows," she said. When his brows lifted, she added, "Minders, the ever-present Gerard."

Josquin shook his head. "I gave him the night off. A bodyguard will follow us, but at a discreet distance. Tonight is for the two of us."

She wasn't sure she wanted that, but a thrill ran down her spine. "Is that safe?" she asked, aware of the exquisite double meaning.

If he heard it, he gave no sign, and a gleaming white Branxton convertible purred to a halt beneath the portico. A servant got out and handed the keys to Josquin. So they were to be truly alone.

"Your car?" she queried as they drove off. The leather upholstery was like butter, the suspension like riding on a cloud. Josquin handled the powerful car with a casual expertise that she couldn't help admiring.

"Leased," he explained. "Guess that makes it my car for now. Like it?"

Feeling the fragrant breeze surround her, she felt more alive than she had in a long time. "Very much. I'm glad Perin persuaded me to let her put my hair up. Otherwise it would be a windblown mess in no time."

He darted her a mischievous look. "Might be a great time-saver."

Did he mean to muss her hair tonight? She shivered, although the night was warm, the stars a million lustrous diamonds far above them. The lights of Valmont city were strung out ahead like more diamonds on a matching necklace. "Josquin," she began unevenly, "Henry won't be around to see us tonight."

He grimaced. "I sincerely hope not."

"Then why must we act romantic?"

"Because it's a fabulous night. I'm with a beautiful woman. What other reason do you need? Besides," he added as if in afterthought, "convincing Henry will be easier the more we stay in character."

For a moment, she'd thought...no, she told herself sternly. He didn't want a real romance, neither did she. Foolish to feel disappointed. "You're right," she said quietly.

She said no more until they arrived at the Royal Yacht Club, perched on a cliff above the harbor. When they were shown into the restaurant, she found that the walls were almost entirely made of glass, and the harbor sparkled at their feet.

Only one table was set, sitting in splendid isolation where they could enjoy the best view. A low light spilled around the table. The other tables were in shadow. She looked around in amazement as the truth dawned. "You booked the entire restaurant for us?"

"I thought you'd be more comfortable if we were alone."

Why not? She was with a member of the royal family, evidenced by the attentive way they were fussed over, menus provided, napkins draped with a flourish.

When the staff withdrew, it was only to a discreet distance where they waited to replenish their glasses after every mouthful. Hardly their fault if she found herself wishing for the reassurance of a crowd around them. Being the focus of Josquin's attention was too unsettling, knowing she craved it, but for her own reasons.

The lowered lights and soft music of a band playing

only for them were powerful reminders of what real romance could have been like with him.

"Hungry?" Josquin asked, his eyes bright.

Her appetite had vanished with the awareness that she had Josquin all to herself tonight. "Not really."

"Would you prefer to dance?"

She wished she had said she was hungry, because the prospect of being held in his arms made her heart flutter madly. But she'd given her answer. Refusing to dance would betray her feelings more surely than if she went along. She nodded and removed the napkin from her lap.

Josquin took her hand and led her to the dance floor. She fumbled the first few steps. "I'm usually better at this," she apologized as her stiletto stabbed his foot. What was the matter with her? She had trained in ballet until she grew too tall to consider a career as a dancer. Now she could barely remember how to put one foot in front of the other.

He pulled her against him and whispered in her ear, "Relax, we're alone here. Just you and me, and the music."

She closed her eyes. Her woven silver Aloys Gada gown was cut almost to the waist at the back, crisscrossed with spaghetti straps that offered no shield against the warmth of the prince's hands on her shoulder and back.

He touched her like a lover, the thought almost snapping her eyes open in alarm. "Keep your eyes closed," he murmured, forestalling her. "Let the music guide you. That's it. My Lord, you're a beautiful dancer. *You're* beautiful, Sarina."

Hearing the huskiness in his voice, she did open her eyes in time to see him looking at her the way a collector might regard a particularly fine addition to his collection.

That's what she was to him, she thought. A trophy, to be collected like those in the cabinet in his office. Futile to imagine she could be anything more.

She didn't want to be anything more, did she?

Her steps almost faltered again, but determination kept her feet moving. She let years of disciplined practice lead her steps, striving to distance herself from the experience, as she had done back home when she had been coerced into a duty dance. She tried to tell herself this was no different. She was dancing with Josquin as much out of duty, as desire.

Except that duty dances had never made her pulse race and her body feel molten, as heat seared through her. She didn't mean to lean into his embrace but she found herself doing it unconsciously. He didn't seem to mind.

She danced with him as if they were one, feeling light enough to float away if he hadn't anchored her to the floor. Distantly she became aware that the staff were watching them, but she no longer cared. Josquin made her feel truly like a princess in his arms, and she never wanted the sensation to end.

The set was a long one, or was it her heightened sensitivity that made the music seem to go on for longer than usual? She felt dazed when the music ended. To the admiring looks of the staff, Josquin led her back to their table.

She ducked her head, embarrassed at the spectacle she must have presented, as if she truly was a woman in love, dancing with the man she desired. Josquin leaned over and tilted her head up, reading the truth in her gaze. "You were magnificent out there."

He was probably glad she had lent such conviction to the fiction of their engagement. "I got carried away," she admitted.

"You weren't the only one."

Josquin was glad she didn't know how much he had wanted to dance her right off the floor, into the elevator and back to his car. He would have driven them somewhere they could be completely alone, no bodyguard, no staff. Then he would have kissed her senseless. Instinct told him he might not have been able to stop at kissing, but what the heck, this was only fantasy, right? He could end it any way he chose.

Hastily he slid the napkin back across his lap, glad of its generous size and weight stopping him from scandalizing the staff. Where Sarah was concerned, his fantasies were fast getting out of hand. He had thought this evening would relax her, help her to carry out the fiction that they were in love. Now he started to wonder how much was fiction on his side.

Confused, he turned his attention to the food. "I took the liberty of ordering a banquet for us," he said, as dish after dish was brought to them on silver salvers. "Having a little of everything saves you having to make difficult choices."

Being around Josquin, difficult choices seemed inescapable, she thought as a waiter offered her a deliciously fragrant shrimp dish. She accepted a tiny portion.

Josquin waited until the man moved away, then frowned. "You're barely eating enough to keep going."

Since her arrival at the château, she had joined him and Prince Henry for several evening meals, but the formal atmosphere made her so uncomfortable that she had found it difficult to eat much of anything. She knew she had lost a few pounds of late. "I'm fine," she insisted.

"And you're doing too much," he went on. "Between meetings with Prince Henry that are more like running battles, your studies in Carramer custom and language, and taking care of Christophe, you'll wear yourself out.''

"Before I came here, I held a full-time job as well,'' she pointed out. "And I didn't have an army of servants to help me.''

"All the same, you will take better care of yourself,'' he said in a tone of royal command she suspected he wasn't aware of using.

She sighed. "Don't think you're going to get away with pushing me around after we're married.''

He seemed to find the idea intriguing. "Convincing you to eat something hardly qualifies as violating your rights, does it?''

He had violated them from the moment they met, she thought. He was still doing it, however unintentionally. When she was with him, her willpower seemed to vanish. She couldn't think of anything except how much she wanted to be in his arms.

Was she falling in love with him against all common sense?

"No!''

She wasn't aware she had exclaimed out loud until Josquin said mildly, "Good, we agree on that at least.''

Paying at least superficial attention to the food allowed her to mull over the unthinkable possibility that she was falling in love with Josquin. In lust, she could accept. Never love. Not when she finally had in her possession the means to leave Carramer—and Josquin—far behind.

She realized he had said something and was awaiting her answer. "Will I be ready for what? I'm sorry, I was distracted.''

"The food isn't that riveting,'' he teased. "I asked

whether you feel up to meeting the rest of the family tomorrow evening.''

She stared at him. ''All of them?'' She had met his royal cousin, Eduard, when she and Josquin were invited to Eduard's villa within the grounds of Château de Valmont. He had made her feel welcome. Josquin's other cousin, Mathiaz, she had met at dinner with Prince Henry. But she had still to meet the monarch, Prince Lorne, and his siblings who lived further afield. Prince Michel and Princess Adrienne had to travel from the neighboring islands, she recalled.

''I'm hosting a cocktail party for my birthday. Most of the royal family will be there, so it will be a perfect time to announce our engagement.''

She masked her dismay. Corbin Rees was due back in Valmont the day after tomorrow. She had hoped she could get Christophe away before Josquin made his announcement. Her departure would cause him enough vexation without the embarrassment of explaining that his bride-to-be had run away.

A piece of shrimp caught in her throat. Or was it guilt at the way she meant to betray Josquin? She swallowed some ice water and her throat cleared, but the guilty sensation remained. She hoped he would eventually find it in his heart to forgive her, because she knew she would be a long time forgiving herself.

''Should you make the announcement so soon?'' she asked shakily.

''Henry is ready to go ahead with his plans for Christophe. Yesterday he told me you're too emotionally involved with him.''

She felt her face drain of color. ''I'm his mother, for goodness' sake. What else should I be?''

''Cold and unemotional, like Henry's own mother. He

revered her as the ideal royal parent. He barely saw her, which is probably why he remembers her as perfect. He wants Christophe brought up the way Henry himself was, schooled in the performance of his royal duty from his first breath.''

''You weren't brought up that way.''

His mouth turned down. ''Mainly because my parents weren't as dutiful as they should have been. Henry didn't get involved in my education until I was a teenager. By then I had developed a mind of my own.''

If he hadn't, she couldn't conceive of caring so much for him, she thought. ''As your experience proves, the old way isn't always best.''

Josquin's hand moved to cover hers. ''Nevertheless, Henry will get his way, unless I make the announcement tomorrow.''

If only she could take Christophe away before the party. But without Corbin Rees's help, she had no hope. ''It seems we have no choice.''

The despair in her tone made him frown. ''You'll probably be more convincing if you don't sound as if you're being sold into bondage.''

Despite his light tone, she heard the hurt behind his words. She wished she could tell him that she wanted to be his wife more than she had any right to want it. She was also afraid that she wanted the one thing he wasn't offering her—his love.

''I'll do my best to play my part,'' she agreed.

The orchestra started up again and Josquin reached for her hand. ''Another dance between courses should help you perfect your performance.''

She moved with him onto the dance floor. She needed no practice in responding to him. What she really needed was an antidote to Josquin's powerful brand of charm.

Chapter Thirteen

Josquin's party was being held in the Pearl Salon, a magnificent room that he had shown Sarah when he gave her a tour of the château soon after she arrived. The room had looked large enough to hold a couple of hundred people, and there seemed to be at least that many gathered together when she was shown in by a uniformed footman.

Her lessons in the Carramer language must be taking effect because she could understand snatches of the conversations taking place around her. She felt too self-conscious to try and speak the language yet, but an equal number of people were chattering in English.

She tried to allay her nervousness by looking around at the priceless furnishings, and Old Masters adorning the walls. On one long wall, French doors had been flung open onto a marble terrace lit by flaming torches. She saw Josquin out there, in conversation with another man in the uniform of a commander in the Carramer Royal Navy. Eduard de Marigny, Marquis of Merrisand, she remembered from their brief meeting in the grounds of the château.

She couldn't believe how much the sight of Josquin reassured her. She could hardly say he calmed her, because the fast beating of her heart belied any such notion. To suit the occasion, he wore a charcoal lounge suit, and to her eye, outshone every other man in the room.

Quite an achievement, she thought, because one of the men was the dashing Prince Lorne himself, monarch of Carramer. He was deep in conversation with a seated Prince Henry and a glamorous woman Sarah recognized as Lorne's consort, Princess Alison.

She was glad now that she had studied the family photo albums Josquin had left with her, because she could mentally put names to many of the faces around her. There was Prince Michel and his wife, Caroline, from the island of Isle des Anges, the flamboyant Princess Adrienne and Sarah's fellow American, Hugh Jordan, now Duke of Nuee, the tiny Carramer island where they lived.

Sarah frowned over the tall man with them, until the name came back to her. He was Mathiaz, Baron Montravel, Josquin's cousin. He had joined Prince Henry for dinner one evening, and had entertained her with descriptions of Josquin as a boy. Being close in age, the two of them had spent a lot of their free time together, mostly getting into mischief, she gathered, although Josquin had denied this.

"You must be our long-lost princess," came a gravelly voice in English at her elbow. She spun around to find herself face to face with a craggy man in his sixties. The twinkle in his eye belied his gruff expression. He held out his hand. "I'm Alain Pascale, court physician to these people, when they'll let me do my job. Mostly they're so disgustingly healthy, that I have to grow orchids to keep myself busy.''

Alain Pascale was a legend in Carramer. She knew he had delivered most of the royal babies for the last couple of generations, and had carte blanche to speak his mind with any of the royal family. His introduction suggested he took full advantage of the privilege.

She took his hand, charmed when he lifted it to his lips. ''Delighted to meet you, Doctor Pascale. I'm Sarah McInnes...I mean de Valmont.''

His eyes narrowed shrewdly. ''Takes some getting use to, I imagine.'' He gestured around. ''Don't let all this pomp and ceremony bother you. They only do it to keep folk like me in our places.''

She felt herself start to relax, as doubtless the doctor had intended. ''Forgive me, but it doesn't seem to be working.''

He smiled and his craggy features assumed a mantle of kindness she suspected that he rarely allowed others to see. ''You and I are going to get along just fine, Princess.''

He lifted a couple of glasses of champagne from the tray of a passing waiter, and handed one to her, then lifted his in a toast. ''I'll look forward to delivering your babies when the time comes.''

When she started to protest, he leaned closer. ''Josquin told me about you two. Don't worry, I'll consider it in confidence until he makes an official announcement. Let me be the first to wish you both all the happiness in the world. He's a fine man, and in my professional opinion, you're just the prescription he needs.''

Lost for words, she was glad when the doctor was called to answer a telephone call. He left her with a murmured apology. At the doctor's confident assertion that she was what Josquin needed, her discomfort had swelled until she could hardly breathe. How could she abandon him now?

She didn't want to, she saw with sudden, blinding clarity. No matter how she tried to ignore it, she was in love with him. Leaving him would be like tearing out her own heart.

Why hadn't she seen it before? She had been so busy assuring herself that she had agreed to marry him for Christophe's sake, that she had failed to see what was crystal clear to her now—she had agreed because she wanted to, because she couldn't imagine her future without Josquin.

She wasn't leaving tomorrow because she couldn't. Somehow she would find a way to return the travel documents to his office before he missed them, then she would play this game out to the end. If it meant marrying the prince when she knew he didn't love her, so be it. She would love him with all her heart, and hope that sometime in the future, he would come to love her back.

If he didn't she would find a way to live with that, too, as long as they could be together. A sob welled in her throat as she contemplated the bargain she was making with herself. She suspected it would be harder to live with than it seemed now. But the alternative, never seeing him again, was far harder.

Worse than hard. Impossible.

So she wouldn't even try. She took a steadying sip of champagne, needing another as soon as she saw Josquin striding toward her.

"You look lovely tonight," he said, then took a closer look. "More than lovely, radiant. As if someone just handed you a miracle."

They had, and his name was Josquin de Marigny. Her heartbeat double-timed as she looked up at him. The uniformed man hovered behind him, obviously impatient to renew their acquaintance.

"You remember my cousin, Eduard de Marigny," Josquin said, sounding reluctant to share her.

"Princess Sarina," Eduard said, bowing over her hand.

"Please call me Sarah," she reminded him.

He kissed her hand in the continental fashion, then spoiled the effect by grinning at Josquin. "Delighted to see you again, Sarah. You have all the luck, Josh."

She stared at Josquin. "Does everyone know?"

He had the grace to look abashed. "I haven't informed Henry yet."

She suspected Josquin had kept their news from Henry because he knew the old prince wouldn't take kindly to hearing it. She could hardly blame him. Josquin's role as Christophe's stepfather would usurp Henry's control over his heir.

She curled her hand into the crook of Josquin's arm, telegraphing her silent support. Whatever storm had to be weathered, she would be there for him from now on. No more doubts or hesitation. She loved him. What more did she need to know?

"Guess we'd better get this over with," he said in an undertone, his hand closing over hers. She saw his back become a fraction straighter and his expression take on a look of determination, as he led her to where Prince Henry was holding court.

The old prince looked better, she saw as they came closer. His color was healthier and he was breathing without the aid of oxygen. She knew his heart could fail at any time, or he could carry on in his present condition for years. He was stubborn enough to do the latter, and she found herself hoping he would, as long as Christophe's future wasn't in his hands.

When Josquin introduced her to Prince Lorne and Princess Alison, Sarah swept them the curtsy she'd been practicing, and was warmed by their sincere welcome and offer of help or advice if needed.

Family, she thought, feeling slightly dazed. They were all her family. She had gone from being a stranger to herself, wondering who her real family might be, to having generations of relatives linked to her by blood or marriage. The long-lost princess, Dr. Pascale had called her. The man was a mind reader, because he had pinpointed exactly how she felt.

Was this why Josquin had been so anxious for her to meet everyone, because he had wanted her to feel this joyous sense of acceptance, of homecoming?

Only one hurdle to their happiness remained, and he was glowering at her now. "What the devil do you mean, you and Sarina are engaged to be married?" Henry demanded. "What will you do if I refuse my permission?"

"I'm afraid you're a little late, Henry," Prince Lorne said smoothly. "When Josh approached me this morning, I gave them my blessing."

The old prince stirred in his chair. "You went to Lorne instead of coming to me?"

"Lorne is the monarch and head of my family. I simply followed protocol," Josquin said easily.

"Maybe, but I've always thought of you as a son. A son comes to his father first."

"Not if the father is going to bite his head off," Lorne pointed out.

"You all think I'm so predictable, don't you? Well

this time, I'm going to surprise you because I'm going to give these two my blessing as well. I recognize when a battle is unwinnable, and I can see one now. You only have to look at these two to see that common sense isn't going to have the slightest effect.''

Was it to be so simple? She could hardly believe that Prince Henry was going to accept their situation so readily. From what she had heard and studied about him, he was a master strategist, a diplomat who could usually manage to get his own way. Josquin must mean a great deal to him, to make him give up something he wanted as badly as he did control of her son.

''Smile, it's all going to work out,'' Josquin whispered in her ear.

She wanted to believe he was right, but couldn't quell her sense of unease. Would she have preferred Henry to rant and rage, she asked herself? He had to be simmering with resentment over being thwarted, yet he looked more like the father of the groom, accepting the congratulations of those around him.

The old prince signaled to an aide who rang a bell for silence. Slowly the hubbub died away and all eyes turned to Henry. Standing at Josquin's side, beside the old prince's chair, she was glad she had dressed with such care for this evening.

From her now extensive wardrobe, she had chosen a simple gown in a Grecian style, draping softly from a cowl neckline. The shimmering, orchid colored fabric dipped low at the back, and skimmed her figure like a second skin, giving her artful curves that the mirror told her were the essence of femininity.

To match her dress, her hair was piled on top of her head, a few curls being allowed to escape to frame her face. As every eye fell on her, she stood straight and proud, buoyed by Josquin's presence at her side.

Earlier in the day, Josquin had personally delivered a pair of exquisite pearl teardrop earrings that he said were heirlooms she was more than entitled to wear. He had also brought her another surprise, a white gold ring set with a flawless diamond in the shape of a heart.

When he had placed the ring on her finger, she hadn't been able to suppress a feeling of excitement, as if he really was pledging his love to her, although she had told herself then that the ring was window dressing, needed for her to play the part of his loving fiancée.

Now she touched the ring for luck and confidence. Josquin saw the slight gesture and smiled at her, all the reassurance she needed. She stood taller, keeping her hand linked through his arm. As long as he stood beside her, who could stand against them?

Prince Henry struggled to his feet, leaning against Josquin's other arm. He surveyed the gathering as a male lion might survey the pride he was duty bound to protect. "Prince Lorne, Princess Alison, honored guests, my family, we're here tonight to celebrate Josquin's birthday, and also to welcome my granddaughter, Sarina, who was lost to us for so long in America, and has now returned to her rightful place among us. Having her back with us means a great deal to me—not least because she has provided Valmont with an heir, the delightful Christophe. I know you will all help them both to feel at home in Carramer."

His voice dissolved into a cough that could have been ill health or an excess of emotion. She suspected the latter. Henry gestured toward Sarah, and she felt herself color as the gathering broke into applause. She inclined her head in what she hoped was gracious acknowledgment, glad of Josquin's hold on her to steady her. She would have to get used to being on public display, she supposed. These people were her family, with her best interests at heart.

Recovering, Henry gestured again for silence. "Not only is it my pleasure to welcome Sarina home, but also to announce another momentous event. You all know the high regard in which I hold Josquin. I have long looked on him as a son, and now he is to become part of my family in fact, when I entrust to him my beautiful granddaughter in marriage." He sat down heavily, chest heaving.

Prince Lorne bent over Henry in concern, but Henry motioned him away. Prince Lorne raised his champagne glass. "I would like to propose a toast to the happiness of Josquin and Sarina."

"To Josquin and Sarina." The murmurs went around the room as glasses were lifted and the toast drunk. Sarah felt Josquin's arm tighten around her in silent agreement. She felt her eyes start to mist and blinked furiously. Princesses didn't cry in public, even if their hearts were overflowing with happiness.

On impulse she leaned down and kissed the old prince. "Thank you, Grandfather."

He waved her away, but she could see his eyes gleaming wetly. She had expected fireworks but the old prince really seemed to be happy for them, she thought in amazement. Perhaps blood really was thicker than water after all.

Soon afterward Henry allowed himself to be taken back to his apartments, although he urged the rest of the family to continue to enjoy the evening. Servants began to weave their way through the room offering trays of appetizing canapés. She even managed to eat a little as

Josquin led her around the room, performing introductions. Everyone was so welcoming, she wondered how she could have felt apprehensive about meeting the rest of the royal family and their close friends.

Suddenly she felt Josquin tense. "Finally," he said, sounding resigned.

She followed his gaze to where a beautiful woman in her mid-fifties was being shown into the room. "Your mother?" she guessed, noting the unmistakable resemblance.

He nodded. "Her Highness, Princess Fleur. Trust her to manage to miss the announcement."

"Surely she wouldn't be late on purpose?"

His mouth tightened. "You don't know my mother. If she isn't going to be the center of attention, she sees no purpose in showing up."

Sarah felt a surge of compassion for him, knowing from experience how hard it was to be at odds with the people you should feel closest to. "Perhaps she'll change once we're married. She might like having a grandchild," she said.

"Perhaps. She loves babies, so she'll be a good grandmother to Christophe, I'll grant her that at least. But she's a handful, so be prepared."

Pleased to hear the hopeful note in his voice, Sarah mentally crossed her fingers that she and Christophe could play a small part in improving relations between mother and son. She watched Fleur sail through the crowd, accepting greetings from the other family members. The woman was the very image of a royal *grande dame,* and Sarah felt a surprising surge of admiration for her.

Mothers-in-law were supposed to intimidate prospective daughters-in-law, Sarah told herself firmly. She hadn't let Henry get the better of her. Compared to him, Josquin's mother should be a dream.

A disturbing dream, she thought, when Josquin performed the introduction. Fleur glared at Sarah over the top of her designer glasses, as if inspecting a riding colt at a sale. "I've only just returned from Paris for my son's birthday, and now I hear you two are engaged to be married. Isn't this rather sudden?"

"Sarina and I are in love," Josquin said.

Fleur made a dismissive gesture. "Am I to understand that you have a child?"

Sarah nodded. "His name is Christophe and he's one year old. Prince Henry has just acknowledged him as the heir to Valmont."

That hit home, she saw, as Fleur's piercing blue gaze flickered. Sarah could almost see the older woman casting herself as grandmother to the heir. If the role made her happy, Sarah couldn't see much harm in it.

"I shall look forward to meeting my future grandson," Fleur said at last.

"You also missed the announcement of my engagement to Sarina," Josquin informed his mother. "Both Lorne and Henry have given us their blessing."

His message was clear. Fleur was not to make their lives difficult. She raised her eyebrows. "Henry approves? I should have thought he would want to manage your child's upbringing himself."

"He trusts Josquin," Sarah said, letting her tone tell Fleur that she did, too.

Fleur gave a sigh. "Then I can do no less. You have my blessing as well." She brightened suddenly. "Being mother of the groom will be such a treat. There's this wonderful new designer in Paris I've been aching to visit. He must design my outfit, and your wedding dress, too, my dear.''

Josquin's expression darkened. ''Mother.''

''Don't use that tone to me, Josquin. You can't mean to penny-pinch when it comes to your own wedding?''

''There's plenty of time to discuss the details. I'll look forward to your help when the time comes,'' Sarah intervened, with a warning look at Josquin. She understood his concern that his mother might see their wedding as an excuse for extravagance he could ill afford, but now wasn't the time to settle the matter. Sarah suspected that Josquin's concern over money was more a matter of pride, borne out of his deprivations as a child, than a real problem.

''I'd better circulate,'' Josquin said, his tone clearly suggesting that the choice was between that and strangling his mother.

''Josquin tells me you live in Solano,'' Sarah said when he left them together. She was glad to move to a less explosive topic of conversation.

Fleur glared at her son's retreating back. ''Exist might be a better word than live, my dear. Josquin is a positive miser when it comes to money, as you'll find out for yourself. Not like his dear father.'' She rolled her eyes. ''I still miss him after seven years.''

A waiter approached them with a tray of delicacies. Fleur inspected them and selected a minute pastry boat filled with caviar.

Sarah said, ''Tell me about Josquin's father.''

It was the right question, she saw as Fleur's expression softened. ''He saw me at a ball one day, when I was lady-in-waiting to his sister-in-law, Charmian, and it was love at first sight. He didn't rest until he had wooed me and made me his princess. Leon was a giant of a man, in character as well as stature.''

"Probably where Josquin gets his strong character from.''

Fleur seemed about to dispute this, until she remembered Sarah's position as mother of the heir. ''You could be right,'' she conceded. ''Of course, he's much harder of heart than his father. Dear Leon could deny me nothing.''

At what cost to Josquin? Sarah wanted to ask, but held her tongue. She didn't want a careless remark to damage her chances of getting along with her future mother-in-law.

Fleur exchanged her empty champagne glass for a full one, and shared a secretive smile with Sarah. ''There are ways a woman can get her own way, my dear.''

"I don't want…''

Fleur waved her to silence. ''Accept some advice from an expert, dear. I wasn't really as surprised as I pretended that Henry gave you his blessing. Before I left for Paris, Henry told me that Josquin was bringing you to Carramer. Henry confided that he hoped you and Josquin would make a match of it.''

Sarah barely kept her confusion from showing. ''He did?''

Fleur nodded. ''Henry told me that if Josquin married you, he would retire the debt on our family estate, and I'd be able to return from my exile in Solano.'' She gave a ladylike shudder. ''My present house has only five bedrooms. Can you imagine? Compared to what Leon meant me to have, I'm in penury.''

"Are you saying Henry bribed Josquin to marry me?'' Sarah asked, every syllable dripping ice.

Fleur shook her perfectly coiffed head. ''Of course

not. More like an inducement. Such things are done all the time in royal circles. And it's not as if you don't want to marry my son. Anyone can see that you're head over heels. I haven't seen him so happy in a long time.''

Why wouldn't he be happy, Sarah thought? She was the only one foolish enough to have fallen in love. On his side, the promise that he would be able to restore his family's wealth ranked as a much greater…what did Fleur call it?…inducement.

Sarah felt dizzy, almost in shock. For the second time in her life she had been bartered to appease a man's ambition. First by James McInnes, so desperate to have a child to satisfy his ego that he hadn't considered the effect on Sarah herself when she found out. She had thought that was as terrible as she could ever feel.

Now Josquin had also treated her as a commodity, to be used for his own ends. Pain throbbed through her, consuming the love for him that had burned like a flame only moments before. She felt utterly betrayed.

Josquin had also betrayed Christophe, she thought. Having ensured that Josquin was beholden to him, Henry could go on controlling her child's life behind the scenes. No wonder Henry had supported the marriage. He had schemed with Josquin and his mother to bring it about.

Why hadn't Josquin told her? Because he knew once all the facts were in her possession, she wouldn't marry him if he was the last prince in Carramer. Cleansing anger washed away her despair, strengthening her as nothing else could have done. She felt her spine straighten and her shoulders slide back. She knew what she had to do.

Fleur studied her in concern. ''You've gone pale, my

dear. Are you quite all right? I haven't spoken out of turn?''

Sarah rallied with an effort and forced a smile. ''You didn't tell me anything I didn't need to know. You've done me a tremendous favor.''

Fleur had stopped her from making the greatest mistake of her life.

Somehow Sarah got through the rest of the evening without betraying that her heart was in little pieces and might never be whole again.

When Josquin kissed her at the door to her suite, she wanted to lash out, to scream at him that she knew what was behind his sudden willingness to marry her, and Henry's unexpected benevolence. But she said nothing, acting the part of the good fiancée while her traitorous body ached with wanting him.

Nerves jittering, she steeled herself to say, ''Tonight I heard that you'll soon have clear title to your family estate.''

Thunder darkened his gaze and she saw his fists clench. ''Mother.''

''So it's true?'' It was all true.

''She shouldn't have told you.''

Sarah touched the back of her hand to his cheek. ''No harm done.'' Or at least not as much as there would have been if she *hadn't* found out. ''You can tell me all about it in the morning.''

''I have business meetings in the morning. We should talk now.''

''It's late.'' And she was holding herself together by a thread. Even now, when he had confirmed his betrayal, she still wanted him. If he came into her suite, she couldn't trust herself not to weaken. Desire was so shameless. She said good-night and carefully closed the door between them.

Not until she reached the sanctuary of her bedroom did she permit herself the indulgence of tears, crying until she felt as if she had no tears left. Then she splashed cool water onto her face to hide the signs of her unhappiness, and started to plan.

Chapter Fourteen

Corbin Rees sounded surprised to hear from her when she telephoned him. "Palace gossip has it that you and Prince Josquin are engaged," he said.

"You shouldn't listen to palace gossip. Is your offer to take me and Christophe back to America still open?"

"Provided you have current travel documents. I can't take a chance on landing in the States and being turned away because of a passenger with no papers."

She thought of the travel documents burning a hole in the bottom of the carryall she had packed with necessities for herself and Christophe. She couldn't carry much without arousing suspicion. The rent had been paid on her apartment in North Hollywood, so they had a home to return to. Everything else would have to wait until she found a job and got back on her feet financially.

Emotionally was another story.

"James McInnes can vouch for us if we need it," she said.

Corbin coughed. "I doubt it. James hasn't been well

lately. I haven't seen him for weeks so I wouldn't count on him for anything.''

''It doesn't matter. Our passports are in order,'' she assured Corbin around the knot in her throat.

''Fine. I'll be landing at Valmont Airport around noon, and taking off again by two. If you're not there...''

''I'll be there,'' she said and closed the connection. She looked around her suite. Perin and Marie had taken Christophe for a walk along the beach. Sarah had been tempted to veto the outing, until she reasoned that the fresh air would help the baby to sleep on the flight.

She should have been having a language lesson but had canceled because of a supposed headache. It was fast becoming a reality. How could she ever have thought herself in love with Josquin?

A sob burst from her throat. She was still in love with him. The blood sizzled through her veins as she thought of his kisses, and the heat of his hands against her skin. Never to know such joy again was almost more than she could endure.

She stiffened her spine. She would have to endure it because the alternative was to let him use her, and she would not be used by anyone ever again.

By the time the ladies-in-waiting returned with Christophe, Sarah was ready. She rebuffed their offers to accompany her, stating that she had arranged to meet Josquin at the airport and he would see her home. She had no idea where his meetings were being held, but neither did Marie and Perin. They accepted her explanation. Perin even volunteered to have a car waiting for her outside, then began to tidy the suite.

Sarah added some of Christophe's things to the hold-all, making it look as if that was the reason she needed the roomy bag. She wasn't accustomed to deception, but maybe being around Josquin, something had rubbed off because her actions were accepted at face value.

She said a silent goodbye to the château as she instructed the chauffeur to take her to the airport. Then she closed the privacy screen between them, not wanting the man to see how hard she was struggling to hold herself together.

Tears gathered behind her eyes as they cruised between the heavy iron gates enclosing the estate. Now that she knew she truly belonged here, she felt as if she was leaving an important part of herself behind.

She blinked furiously and focused on Christophe, kicking happily in his baby seat. "We're going home, sweetheart," she crooned to him. "Everything will soon be all right, I promise."

But how could she make such a promise when her breaking heart warned her that nothing in her life would be all right ever again?

The royal standard fluttering from the car afforded the limousine unchallenged entry into the airport surrounds, and they were able to pull up alongside Corbin's private jet. She pulled in a steadying breath. This was the hardest part. Once they were airborne, she would feel much better. She couldn't feel any worse.

Corbin came down the steps to meet the car, and held the door open before the chauffeur could get to it. "Are you sure you're doing the right thing?" he asked.

In the act of releasing Christophe from his seat, she looked back. "You sound nervous, Corbin. You're only giving a friend a lift, not breaking any laws."

He took her arm. "Look, before you go on board, I should tell you…"

If he restrained her much longer, she wouldn't have

the courage to go at all, so she moved free of his grasp. "Please don't lecture me, Corbin. I'm not feeling too well right now. Tell me later how stupid I am to throw all this away, but don't try to stop me now."

She lifted Christophe into her arms and handed the carryall to Corbin, then made her way up the steps and into the next stage of her life.

She hadn't planned on finding Josquin seated in one of the armchairs in the lounge area of the plane. Her heart turned over at the sight of him. Not now, her mind screamed. Couldn't he see that this was hard enough, without him making it more difficult by trying to pretend he wanted her to stay?

"Hello, Sarina," he said quietly. Corbin backed away and disappeared into the cockpit.

She settled Christophe into one of the seats and fastened a seat belt around him to prevent him from rolling off, then tucked his toy horse in beside him. The baby was sleepy after his morning on the beach. His eyes closed before he could reach for the toy. Envy gripped her. If only she could close her eyes on Josquin and sleep until she was far away from him.

But he remained as large as life behind her, patiently waiting until she had taken care of the baby. When she turned, she surprised a look of such anguish on his face that she felt shaken to her core. Surely he only cared because she affected his deal with Prince Henry?

"What are you doing here?" she asked wearily.

"Evidently saying goodbye to my fiancée."

Bitterness welled inside her, warring with the urge to take his face in her hands and kiss away the anguished look that was tearing her apart. "I was never your fiancée, except in name. And even that turned out to be a set-up to help you get your land back."

"You believed what my mother told you?"

"You confirmed it yourself last night."

"I agreed I was close to regaining unencumbered title of the estate. Until I spoke to my mother this morning, I didn't know you thought I'd achieved it through making a deal with Henry."

Sarah shot him a bleak look. "Fleur told me such inducements are common in royal marriages."

"Not in my marriage."

His thunderous denial made her flinch. He saw her recoil from him, and stood up, gathering her into his arms. She refused to yield, although everything in her wanted to. "Are you telling me there was no agreement?"

"Before I met you, Henry did offer to buy the title back for me if I married you and allowed him to control Christophe's future. He even enlisted my mother to try to persuade me," he said evenly. As she looked away, he added, "But I turned him down."

Gently he brought her head back around so she had no choice but to meet his dark gaze. "Did you hear me? I turned him down flat."

Confusion roiled through her. "But you have reclaimed your estate."

"By my own efforts. Do you remember the floating baby seat Christophe so loved using in the pool? I designed it to entertain my cousins' children. A manufacturer saw it and offered to market it on a profit sharing basis."

"You're Jaydem?" she said, astonishment in her voice.

"My initials," he confirmed. "The seat won an international award and has never looked back. The factory produces the millionth Jaydem seat next month. I'm using my share of the royalties to retire the debt on the estate. Now do you understand?''

''I understand that I've been a complete fool,'' she confessed. ''I was so in love with you, that thinking you and Henry were in league against me almost destroyed me.''

His fingers tangled in her hair. ''Say that again.''

''About Henry?''

''About loving me.''

''I do love you. I know you don't want to hear it, but it's the truth.''

His breath gusted between them. ''You can't know how much I've longed to hear it, but I told myself I had no right to your love until I had more to offer you.''

Rocked to her core, she clung to him, drawing on his strength to hold her upright. ''I never wanted material things from you. When I agreed to marry you, my dearest hope was that you would someday come to love me back.''

''Someday happened the day I set eyes on you,'' he said, his voice husky.

''Although you hardly knew me?''

''You're forgetting I had your photographs beside me for months.''

She gave a choked laugh. ''Serves you right for spying on me.''

''What punishment do you think I deserve?''

She pretended to think. ''A life sentence at the least.''

His heated gaze roved over her. ''You'd better mean the kind that starts with wedding vows? Because I'll accept nothing less as my sentence, my darling Sarina.''

Her eyes blurred but with happiness this time, as she pressed a kiss to his mouth. He tried to capture her lips and she was more than willing, but there was more she wanted to say. "You realize there will be no possibility of parole?"

His eyes danced. "Not even for good behavior?"

She tried to sound severe and failed. "Somehow, I doubt the behavior you have in mind can be called good."

"At least give me credit for waiting until we're married," he said in mock offense. Then he frowned. "Say you'll marry me, for real this time, Sarina. Not for Christophe or for Henry, but because I love you so much I can't think of living without you."

Her heart sang with joy. "Christophe and Henry will be part of our lives," she pointed out.

"I shall love Christophe as my own son, and attend Henry as long as he is ruler of Valmont, but he'll have no say in our family life, I promise you."

She could ask for no more. "I'll marry you, Josquin. I love you with all my heart."

A discreet cough from the cockpit heralded Corbin's return. "I hate to interrupt Your Highnesses, but it's time we took off. I take it you're not coming with me?"

Josquin held her tightly against him. "Sorry Rees, Sarah and Christophe are coming with me."

Corbin gave an embarrassed grin. "Don't be sorry. I had no idea what I was going to do with her anyway."

Josquin's look told her he knew exactly what he was going to do as soon as they were married. She rested her head against his shoulder, reveling in the feel of padded muscle and the bedrock certainty that, whatever he did, she was going to love it.

Epilogue

She always got nostalgic on Christmas Eve, Sarah thought. Even in a tropical country like Carramer, where the sky remained blue and the sun shone fit to burst, she kept up the old traditions. They still decorated a tree, although it was ironwood instead of a fir tree, and the chef produced turkey and plum pudding to jostle with lobster and chilled tropical fruits.

A rattle at her side caught her attention. Christophe had toddled up with a large gaily wrapped parcel, and was shaking it vigorously. She took it from his protesting hands. "Soon, sweetheart. We'll open our presents as soon as the others get here."

"Daddy home?" the two-year-old asked hopefully.

Her eyes misted. "Yes, sweetheart, Daddy will be back from America in time for presents." She would have dearly loved to go with him, but at six months pregnant, he hadn't wanted her to make the long flight, assuring her she would be bored with the royal business he had to attend to.

She probably would have been, but she would have endured the boredom for the joy of stolen moments in a hotel suite, when he could have held her in his arms, instead of arousing her with unbearably romantic telephone calls that left her aching for his touch.

This would be her second Christmas in Carramer. The last year had been filled with the joy of their wedding and now the new baby, and then sadness with the passing of Prince Henry.

He had grumbled that Christophe's upbringing was anything but royal, but grudgingly acceded to their wishes. She saw for herself that her child was happy. When he grew into his role as ruler of Valmont, he would be in touch with his people, having lived and been educated among them. She could think of no better training for him.

For all Henry's cantankerous manner, she missed her grandfather, regretting that they'd had so little time to get to know one another. She was glad he had rallied enough to escort her down the aisle, although he had done so in a wheelchair. A month after they returned from their honeymoon in Australia, Henry had passed away peacefully in his sleep, his ailing heart simply giving out.

She had Josquin and Christophe, and a new baby on the way, she told herself to dispel the sadness. Josquin was a fine Crown Regent. His experience of struggle and want in his own life had stood him in good stead when it came to governing the province. And he was the most attentive husband that any woman could desire. Sharing him with his country was a small price to pay for the happiness he brought her every day they were together.

Her heart leaped as she heard his limousine pull up outside the house. Château de Valmont remained the royal residence, but they spent as much time as they could at Josquin's estate on the outskirts of the city.

She loved the quiet, rural beauty of the place. Even when Josquin's mother was at home, which was seldom since she preferred spending time in Paris, their houses were far enough apart that Sarah didn't feel smothered by her mother-in-law. She had developed a sneaking admiration for the lady-in-waiting turned princess. Auntie Mame had nothing on Fleur, Sarah thought.

Christophe raced to the window and pressed his nose to the glass. "Daddy! Daddy!"

Sarah stood up, sharing Christophe's enthusiasm. She missed Christophe calling Josquin Osh, but daddy sounded just as wonderful. Her heart picked up speed at the prospect of seeing Josquin again. Her welcoming smile faltered as she saw the two people who followed him into the room.

"Rose? James?" Her adoptive parents were the last people she had expected. James looked as if he had aged a decade since she last saw him, and Rose was thinner, with violet shadows rimming her eyes.

Rose gave her a shaky smile. "I know this is a shock, Sarah. Josquin wanted to surprise you."

He had certainly done that. The last time she had seen them, James had ordered her to choose between him and finding her birth parents. She had left home under that cloud, and hadn't returned even when she was pregnant with Christophe.

"Say something please, darling," Rose begged. "I've so longed to see you again. Josquin told us about your father, and Christophe."

"You didn't come to our wedding," Sarah said stiffly. So many breaches had been healed with her marriage to Josquin that she had decided it was time to take the first step with her adoptive parents. Their refusal, although warm enough, still rankled.

Rose looked away, then back at Sarah, her eyes filling. "James was ill with a perforated ulcer. For a time, we thought he might not recover and when he did, we thought you were better off without us. We didn't tell you because we didn't want to spoil your happiness."

"We felt we'd done enough of that already," James added gruffly. "I shouldn't have told you to choose between us and your real parents. If you'd known all along that you were adopted, it wouldn't have been such a shock to you, but I let my ego get in the way. I wanted you to be my child and nobody else's. I'm sorry."

Tears gathered in her eyes as she went to him. Enfolding her was a little tricky, given her pregnant state, but James managed to hold her and dry her tears just as he'd done when she was a little girl. Extricating herself, she hugged Rose, too, feeling the wounds they had inflicted on her start to hurt a little less.

"I brought someone else to spend Christmas with us," Josquin said, sounding strained.

She turned to him, blanching as she saw the woman framed in the doorway. She was slighter than Sarah remembered, her hair tinged with gray. But Sarah would have recognized her anywhere. "Juliet?" Sarah's voice came out as a strangled whisper. "Oh my stars, Juliet."

The woman took a few faltering steps into the room. "Yes, it's me. I never thought I'd see you again, and now you're all grown up and a princess. You're every bit as beautiful as I imagined."

James coughed. "Juliet wanted to tell you who you were, and I wouldn't let her. That's why she left."

Sarah nodded, overcome with emotion. She had last seen Juliet when she was a child. Now her bewildered gaze went from Juliet Coghlan, her birth mother, to Josquin. "But how...where..."

"After we were married, I asked Peter Dassel to track Juliet down in Australia. It took a year, but he finally found her running a business library in Hobart, Tasmania."

Peter was originally from Australia, Sarah recalled. He would have the contacts to find someone there, if anybody could. She understood why Josh hadn't wanted her to accompany him to America this time. She crammed a hand to her mouth. "I can't believe this."

Juliet held out her arms. "Can you forgive me for giving you away?"

Sarah went into the embrace, her heart racing. "You thought my father didn't want us."

"Josquin told me Philippe died without knowing you existed. I wanted so much to tell you I was your mother but..."

"But I was too much of a stubborn fool," James repeated. "If you want us to leave, we'll understand, as long as you know how sorry we are about everything."

Sarah disentangled herself from her mother, stayed within touching distance of both women. From having no mother, she now had both her birth mother and her adoptive mother together. Christmas was indeed a time for miracles.

"None of you is going anywhere," she said in her most regal tone, learned from Prince Henry. Inside, she felt like a small child at Christmas, given a present she had never dreamed of receiving.

The part of her that had felt empty overflowed with love and joy. She had a second chance to get to know her real mother, adoptive parents who cared about her after all, and her wonderful, miraculous Josh, as well as their precious Christophe and the new baby. She could hardly speak for the emotions welling inside her.

Josh spoke for her. "You have a lot of catching up to do, and the whole Christmas holiday to do it."

James's face seamed with concern. "Can you forgive me, Sarah?"

She struggled to find her voice. "When I became a mother myself, I forgave you, James. I learned that having a child can drive you to extremes of behavior. Having you all here makes Christmas perfect."

"Presents now?"

She looked down to find Christophe at her knee, hopefully holding out another wrapped gift. "Yes, presents now," she said, laughing through tears of happiness. On this night, she had received enough gifts to last her a lifetime, but she could see she wasn't going to convince a two-year-old of that when there were real presents to be opened.

"Happy, darling?" Josquin asked much later, when she sat cradled in his arms on the sofa.

Christophe was tucked up in bed, a new toy horse clutched in his arms. James, Rose and Juliet had also retired to their rooms. Sarah felt emotionally and physically exhausted, but she had never felt more at peace.

"How could I not be happy?" she said. "Thank you for giving me the best Christmas surprise in the world. I never expected to see my real mother again."

He kissed the top of her head. "Christmas is a time for surprises."

"I haven't given you anything to compare with what you've given me."

"The day you agreed to become my wife you gave me everything I ever wanted," Josquin said, love ringing in his voice. He stood up and stretched. "We should get some sleep, too. Mathiaz and Eduard are joining us for breakfast.''

"How are they?'' She hadn't seen as much of them as she had wished, since the family came together for the reading of Prince Henry's will. The time had flown as she and Josh settled into their new role, not to mention making a beautiful royal baby.

"They're both well. Jealous of us.''

"Perhaps we ought to start matchmaking for them.''

"I doubt if my cousins would appreciate the help. Mathiaz made enough cynical remarks when he discovered that Henry had bequeathed him Antoinette's wedding ring. Legend says the ring brings true love to whoever possesses it.''

"Doesn't he want to find true love?''

Josquin took her hand and helped her to her feet, pulling her against him. "Mathiaz has yet to discover what you and I know, that true love is the most precious gift in all the world.''

Her radiant expression revealed her wholehearted agreement. "I hope the ring works its magic for Mathiaz soon. And Eduard, too.'' She liked both her royal cousins and wanted the best for them.

Josquin slanted her an amused look. "Henry left Eduard a hunting lodge. How is that supposed to help his love life?''

She offered her husband a radiant smile. "I don't know, but I'm sure it will. Pregnant princesses know these things.''

"Then Eduard better watch out. You're one pregnant princess I wouldn't want to argue with.''

"You're only saying that because I can't outrun you at the moment.''

He planted a loving kiss on her parted lips. "Who

says I want to? Come on, pregnant princess, let's go to bed."

She was out of shape for curtsying but she tried anyway, laughing as he saved her from tumbling over.

"Bed sounds wonderful," she agreed. With Josquin it always did.

* * * * *

Will the ring work on Mathiaz?
Find out next month in
THE BARON & THE BODYGUARD
Valerie Parv's next story in
THE CARRAMER LEGACY!

Silhouette Romance presents tales of
enchanted love and things beyond explanation
in the heartwarming series

Soulmates

Couples destined for each other are brought
together by the powerful magic of love....

Legends come alive in
HER LAST CHANCE
by DeAnna Talcott (on sale November 2002)

Broken hearts are healed
WITH ONE TOUCH
by Karen Rose Smith (on sale January 2003)

Love comes full circle when
CUPID JONES GETS MARRIED
by DeAnna Talcott (on sale February 2003)

Soulmates

Some things are meant to be....

*Available at
your favorite retail outlet.*

COMING NEXT MONTH

#1624 SKY FULL OF PROMISE—Teresa Southwick
The Coltons
Dr. Dominic Rodriguez's fiancée ran out on him—and it was all Sky Colton's fault! Feeling guilty about the breakup, Sky reluctantly posed as Dom's finacée to calm his frazzled mother. But would their pretend engagement lead to a real marriage proposal?

#1625 HIS BEST FRIEND'S BRIDE—Jodi O'Donnell
Bridgewater Bachelors
Born in the same hospital on the same day, Julia Sennett, Griff Corbin and Reb Farley were best friends—until romance strained their bonds. Engaged to Reb, Julia questioned her choice in future husbands. Now Griff must choose between his childhood buddy…and the woman he loves!

#1626 STRANDED WITH SANTA—Janet Tronstad
Wealthy, successful rodeo cowboy Zack Lucas hated Christmas—he didn't want to be a mail-carrying Santa and he certainly didn't want to fall in love with Jenny Collins. But a brutal Montana storm left Zach snowbound on his mail route, which meant spending the holidays in Jenny's arms...!

#1627 THE BARON & THE BODYGUARD—Valerie Parv
The Carramer Legacy
Stricken with amnesia, Mathiaz de Marigny didn't remember telling his beautiful bodyguard that he loved her—or that she had refused him. Now Jacinta Newnham vowed a new start between them. But what would happen when the truth surrounding Mathiaz's accident—and Jacinta's connection to it—surfaced?

#1628 HER LAST CHANCE—DeAnna Talcott
Soulmates
Looking for a spirited filly with unicorn blood, foreign heiress Mallory Chevalle found no-nonsense horse breeder Chase Wells. According to legend, his special horse could heal her ailing father and restore harmony to her homeland. But could a love-smitten Mallory heal Chase's wounded heart?

#1629 CHRISTMAS DUE DATE—Moyra Tarling
Mac Kingston was a loner who hadn't counted on sharing the holidays—or his inheritance—with very beautiful, very wary and very pregnant Eve Darling. But when she realized she'd found the perfect father—and husband!—could she convince Mac?